From the Ashes of Courage

An Ardor Point Novel

J. Timothy King

Back cover: Sunset at Merepoint, ME. Photograph by Carol Blyberg.

From the Ashes of Courage
(Ardor Point #1)

Copyright © 2010 J. Timothy King. All rights reserved.

Published by J. Timothy King.
More content at `http://www.JTimothyKing.com/`

First paperback edition, February 2010.
ISBN 978-0-9816925-4-8

Printed in the United States of America.

10 9 8 7 6 5 4 3 2 1

To certain women of my past, and the painful realities that taught me to appreciate the kind of love offered without strings.

Chapter One

*G*ail Bishop eased open the door and basked in the newness as it washed over her. She had visited the suite only once before, when she and Ann had set it up last week, every last piece of furniture in place. Very little in the room, in fact, they had bought new. New paint, and the air still smelled of it. New, colorful posters lined the walls. A new telephone, new stapler, new office supplies. But the desks, file cabinets, office partitions they had purchased on the used market—complete with scratches in the paint and nicks on the corners—from among the many poor businesses that had been going under. The computers they had gotten off eBay and craigslist. Even in the diagnostic meeting room, set off with a closed door for privacy, the children's picture books they used there, their nasometer and other specialized diagnostic equipment, almost all of it they managed to find pre-owned.

But it all felt new to Gail. And that's what she had told Ann, but Ann didn't seem to understand.

She had started a business only once before, and at the time it excited and sickened her. Excited her, because she had known she was accomplishing something that mattered, because she would make a happy difference for untold hundreds of children. Sickened her, because she had known she could fail.

That was then, this was now. This time the newness almost felt familiar, comfortable. But despite the fact that her future did not hold the uncertainty, it still excited her beyond mere words. Because even though she knew where to look, there was still the seeking. And in the seeking, there lived her passion.

When she had told Ann this, the sweet, sensitive blonde replied with a vacant smile, that "I know what you're saying is a profound revelation to you, but I just don't get it" expression. Gail appreciated her fortune in landing her as a business partner. That was new, too: Gail had never had a business partner before. Ann's unmitigated kindness and infinite patience made her an excellent speech-language pathologist, though a novice businesswoman. But Gail had confidence that she would soon get it.

"You going in? Or you just gonna stand there and admire the place?"

Gail recognized Ann's voice from behind her. She turned and beamed at her new business partner.

"You look happy," Ann said, smiling back politely.

She and Gail stood opposite each other like black and white, literally as well as figuratively. Gail's curly, raven hair was always poufing out in the wrong direction; Ann's straight, blonde hair seemed to trickle like water over her shoulders. Gail stayed inside out of the sun, because otherwise her ghost-like skin would fry up like a strip of bacon; but Ann always looked tanned. Gail looked out from behind brown eyes, and her eyebrows, though well-defined, were too straight and flat, almost like a man's; meanwhile, Ann's blue eyes stuck out, the most dazzling feature on her flawless face, because of the arch of her pale brows. Gail always watched calories, because they always turned her thighs into lamb shanks; Ann's super-model figure never wavered, no matter how much or what she ate. Gail had barreled her way through school through single-mindedness and hard work, and as a result she rarely dated; in school, Ann had always had a thing going with some guy or other, and she almost never studied. And after Ann graduated with honors and passed her certification on the first try, she married a simple but genuinely attractive man, worked for a couple years, then had kids and dropped out of the workforce. Now she was looking to get started again. Gail couldn't even imagine living a life like that.

Despite their differences, the two women had become fast friends from the moment they met in a graduate course on voice disorders. Gail didn't understand why or how it had happened. They had said "Hello" one day, began chatting, started spending time together. And no matter how much distance came between them, physical or emotional, they remained fast friends.

So when Gail's business in Worcester started to bore her, and she began looking for a change, she turned operations over to Clarice, her friend and manager there, and she moved back into the Boston area, to team up with Ann in a new venture.

"I love this!" Gail gushed. "It's like— Like you're finally free."

Ann nodded politely.

"Like nothing can hold you back. You know what I mean?"

"I know," Ann said. "You said that before." She was smiling, half with joy, Gail was sure, but half from how silly Gail must have seemed to her. Gail knew, because she had been there before.

Ann continued. "You looked lonely for a long time, every time I saw you. It's good to see you this way again, like the person I remember from back in college. It's the first time you've seemed happy since you moved back. You should go out more," Ann said. "Go out and meet new people—"

Gail interrupted. "I don't think we'll have time for much going out, Ann. There's too much work to do."

Ann sighed. "Yeah, I get that. But just one night, after work. I mean, we're not going to be working all the time, are we?"

"Pretty much," Gail said, "at first."

"You can't spare time for just one date? Come on. Bob

has a friend who'd love to meet you."

Suddenly, it struck Gail what was going on. A blind date. She shook her head. "Ann," she said. "I don't go on blind dates. You know I don't go on blind dates. I've never gone on blind dates."

"*You* never go on *any* dates," Ann said. "And I know you. You *can* make time to take a night off."

"I don't need a guy in my life right now," Gail said.

"This isn't about a relationship. It's about having fun once in a while, so you don't implode."

"Well, I don't need any fun, either."

"He's a nice guy."

"Not interested," Gail sang, walking toward her desk.

Ann followed. "His name's Eddie. He's good-looking, easy-going, fun to be with, and he won't try any funny stuff, I guarantee it."

"How do you know?" Gail asked, facing her friend across the desk.

"Well," Ann reconsidered, "not unless you want him to."

"This is ridiculous!" Gail was reaching the end of her patience. She sat and turned her attention to some papers on the desk. She didn't care *which* papers, as long as they served as a distraction from Ann's hassling.

"Okay, so he likes to date," Ann said, "a lot. But he's a gentle guy, and he won't take advantage of you. Not unless you want to, anyhow."

Gail leered at her.

"Sweetie," Ann said, "you have to loosen up a little!"

Gail returned to her fake paperwork.

Ann sat on the edge of Gail's guest chair. "I'm going to keep badgering you," she said, grinning, "until you give in. So you might as well agree right now and save us both a lot of annoyance."

"Why do you do this to me?" Gail said. "You did it in college—"

"I never did it while you were married," Ann corrected her.

"I don't want to talk about that," Gail said. "And you've done it every time I've visited since then."

"It's in my nature, and you're my friend, and I'm tired of seeing you lonely all the time."

"You want me to have sex with a stranger."

"I just want you to meet someone, who's fun to be with. And he is. Have a good time. The rest is up to you."

Gail said nothing.

"I promise," Ann added.

Still silence.

"Please?" Ann put on a pouty expression.

Gail took a deep breath and sighed it out. "Okay. Just one date. But then will you leave me alone and let me work?"

"Yes!" Ann beamed from ear to ear.

"But," Gail added, "I won't promise to have fun."

———

I married George Edward Chase when I was very young, only 22 years old. I divorced him when I was even younger. We were only married for 3 years, just a little longer than it took for me to get my master's degree and my first real job.

But by the time I had been offered that job, it was clear we had both made a huge mistake. Our differences were preventing us from finding our way together.

I had been offered an exciting entry-level position at a speech-therapy clinic in Worcester. George wanted to move to Hull so he could live on the beach. George loved the beach. That's how he was, a free spirit, like the water, washing over the sand as it wills, then going out to sea—and who knows where it goes. At first, I thought it was silly, to move somewhere just to be near the beach. But I saw that he was serious, and there was no way I was going to commute from Hull to Worcester every day.

This was just the last in a long line of situations that drew us farther and farther apart. We never could have made it together, two incompatible people in two incompatible places, in a marriage of convenience, which is no real marriage at all.

"We should never have gotten married," I told him. "I knew I wanted to work on my career. We both knew. Now, we're living two separate lives."

Maybe it sounds silly to some, to break up a marriage

over an hour-and-a-half on the Interstate. But for us, divorce would resolve the true conflict, the distance that had seeped into our marriage.

"We should never have gotten married," I repeated.

When I said it, he stared at me with sad, soulful eyes the color of sand, and I finally understood. Every time I had told him I had to work or study, instead of spending time with him, hanging out with his friends, socializing, or whatever else he wanted me to do... Every time my schooling had gotten in the way, he had stared at me with those same, empty eyes, and they had always confused and disturbed me. I only realized at the end of the road that meaning—not emptiness—filled them, because in them reflected the signposts of our destination.

I intoned the magic words, "I want a divorce."

He never told me that I made him sad, and I didn't ask. He didn't say anything. We didn't fight. By then, we didn't fight about anything anymore.

He nodded silently. But his eyes spoke volumes.

"I'm so sorry," I said.

I've always done whatever I had to, whatever needed to be done. I've always stuck with it, followed the road to the very end. I've always searched until I found the pot of gold at the end of the rainbow, no matter what challenges I've faced along the way.

But somehow, it never seems to get any easier.

Chapter Two

*E*ddie reached across the lunch table for the check. Unfortunately, Bob had sprung faster today, or at least that's how the situation appeared to an untrained observer.

Eddie, on the other hand, had used that very trick plenty of times, to distract attention at just the right moment. Bob had asked a simple question: where was the men's room? And Eddie never suspected that Bob actually knew ahead of time that it was "over there and around the corner," until Bob had staked his claim to pay the bill.

"Nuh uh," Eddie said matter-of-factly, holding out his hand. "It's my turn."

"Are you kidding?" Bob almost laughed. "You've gotten it the last *three* times, at least. Actually, I've lost track."

"But it's my pleasure," Eddie countered, his eyes sparkling with a smile, "one of the last few pleasures I have in life."

"That's a pleasure you can do without, what with the way the market's been."

"Don't remind me," Eddie said. He snapped his fingers, as though by sheer insistence he could intimidate Bob into handing over the check.

Bob's prominent proboscis gave his face just enough
character to appear authentic, as authentic as he actually
was. Other than that, he appeared likeable. Short, dark
hair; baby face; an approachable aura surrounding him,
reflecting his friendly personality. Eddie had to go out of
his way to make people like him as much as they naturally liked Bob. Eddie wore a modern-looking chin strip
and mustache, to highlight the freewheeling, easy-going
nature he wished he could portray. He always stowed his
glasses in his pocket—unless he was driving—because
they were so un-cool. And he butted friendly heads with
people like Bob, who occasionally insisted on outdoing
him.

Eddie snapped his fingers again at his friend. "Come
on," he urged, nervousness and annoyance leaking into
his voice, despite the friendly demeanor he tried to
muster.

"Come on, what?" Bob said.

"Come on, *sir,*" Eddie said, knowing Bob would get a
kick out of the joke.

"Ba dum bum," Bob intoned, chuckling. He took a
breath and stared Eddie in the eye. "Do you know that
you're getting annoying."

"Sorry," Eddie said, "but you're stepping on my turf,
and I'm getting antsy." He raised his eyebrows in mock
indignation.

"Okay," Bob said. "I'll let you pay on one condition."

"Name it!" Eddie replied, feeling more at ease already.

"Take out my wife's old, college girlfriend."

"Done," and Eddie reached for the check.

"On a date." Bob apparently thought the request required clarification.

"Sure," Eddie said. "That's what I thought you meant."

"That's it?" Bob pulled back, as if he expected there was more to it. "You'll just 'take her out'?"

"Sure," Eddie said. "Why not? Is there something wrong with her?"

Bob shook his head. "No, nothing. She's beautiful, smart, successful, the whole bit."

"Then I don't see the problem." Eddie reached again for the check, just before Bob snatched it away again.

"The problem is that this is a favor for Ann."

"So?" Eddie didn't know what that meant. "I like Ann. Is there some reason I shouldn't do Ann a favor?"

"Not you," Bob explained, "but maybe Gail."

"Gail?" Eddie asked.

"Yes, that's her name. Gail."

"I knew a Gail once," Eddie stared up into the ceiling, reminiscing about the only woman who ever broke his heart. "She also was beautiful and smart and successful." His face fell a little.

"Well, *this* Gail," Bob said, "she probably feels pressured, and she may not actually want to go out with you. She might not be much fun."

"Okay." Eddie got it now. The date might be a chore. But Eddie could still make the best of it. "So what does she like to do?"

"Work."

"Besides work." Eddie grimaced.

"I don't know."

"Well, don't you think we ought to find out?"

"Gail just said to meet her at Basilio's."

Eddie grinned. "Basilio's?" He said it with an Italian accent. "Nice!" She had good taste, or someone did.

"And wear a white daffodil in your lapel," Bob added.

"You're kidding."

Now Bob grinned, an almost evil smile. "No, I'm not." He handed Eddie the check.

———

Gail stood waiting at the restaurant, twirling a white daffodil between her fingers, a silly, corny form of identification, but sweet at the same time. A mural covered the interior walls, as though looking out from an Italian villa onto the Colosseum and the Arch of Constantine on one side, St. Peter's Basilica on the other. She wondered about the scent, maybe oregano, with other flavors. Her stomach began to growl. Outside, cars drove by in the darkness.

Maybe she had been stood up. Or maybe he had already been here, seen her, and changed his mind. She giggled at the thought. That's okay. She could always open box 237 and take him out of his envelope. She didn't want to be here anyhow; being stood up didn't seem so bad.

The front door opened, and Gail's jaw nearly dropped on the floor. It had been over five years, and he was wearing a charcoal-grey suit, a peach shirt and tie, too dressy for him, probably because of the restaurant. He wore a small beard and mustache; that was different. But it was definitely the same man she had once known, now standing before her. Handsome, delicate glasses sat on a straight nose, framing eyes of bright brown, almost tan-colored, with sharp, black pupils that ripped through her soul. Those eyes made her marry him, and ultimately divorce him, too.

He scanned the room, noticed Gail, lifted off his glasses, slid them into his breast pocket. "Gail," he said, welcoming, friendly.

She sent back to him a warm, welcoming smile that made his heart jump in anticipation.

"George!" she said. "What are you doing here?"

"I think I'm looking for you," he said, holding up a white daffodil.

Her gut did a double-take, then her mind. *How did this happen?* She considered a possibility that angered her with suspicion.

"Did you set this up?" she asked.

"Set what up?"

"This date. The names. The flowers. Everything." Her

anger was building, and she knew she was making less and less sense.

"Bob told me it was Ann's idea," Eddie said, still smiling, hiding his nervousness. He wanted to calm her down. "I didn't know you knew her."

"Then why the fake name?"

"What fake name?"

"Eddie," she said.

"That's my name. That's what people call me. My *middle* name."

George *Edward* Chase, Gail remembered.

She shook her head and wanted to say something, but confusion had overtaken her anger.

"If I had known you were in town," he continued, "I would have simply asked you to get together. Sneaking around, that's not my style."

It was true. George didn't have to connive to make friends, and he let people be who they were. She might have disappointed him by turning down his invitation, but he wouldn't have schemed, not like this.

"So," Gail said, "this is really just an accident."

"Well," Eddie said, "a coincidence." He thought again. Maybe the word *accident* could work. "A *happy* accident."

Eddie saw her beginning to relax, and he responded in kind. Even though she had broken his heart, the sight of her brought him joy. She stared at him, as beautiful as ever, had not aged a day in the last decade. Or maybe the light was just playing tricks on his eyes, or his eyes playing tricks on the light. He gazed upon her face, pale with dark lines, still took his breath away, pierced his heart. The softness of her jaw, her neck, sometimes she revealed them by pulling her thick, curly, black hair together in a ponytail. Tonight, she left it loose, and that was beautiful, too.

He had thought of her often, had already accepted that he would never get over her, that she would probably always mean something special to him. But he had always imagined anxiety, hurt, strain, maybe even anger or hatred, if he saw her again. He had never expected to feel this at ease.

"So," Gail said, as if beginning a sentence.

George seemed genuinely happy to see her, and he would probably be up for dinner. But she didn't know how she felt about it. She didn't hate him, despite the falling out they had shared. It was just one of those things. But he had taken the breakup pretty hard, and she had never contacted him again, nor responded to his infrequent messages, because she didn't want to break his heart any more than she already had. She didn't consciously shun him, didn't mean to blow him off, but something more important had always gotten in the way, something more urgent than dealing with her feelings about George. And the longer she had put him off, the easier it became. She probably would never have come to this dinner, no matter how it affected Ann, if she had known who she was going to meet here, because something more important would have gotten in the way.

She always had a soft spot in her heart for this man, and she probably always would. But it saddened her that they couldn't make it work between them.

And it was definitely dangerous for them to be dating.

"So," Eddie interrupted Gail's thoughts by continuing her own sentence, "do you want to get a table?"

"I'm not sure this is a good idea," she replied.

"Dinner? Why not?" He knew what she was aiming at, but he was playing it cool, as if being with her was no big deal.

"I'm not sure it's a good idea for us to..." She couldn't say the word *date*. It just felt... weird.

"To eat? To sit?" Eddie pretended to think for a moment. "To dance? There's no room in here to dance, and everyone would look at us funny, so... yeah, you're probably right."

Gail giggled, which loosened her up. "To date."

Eddie smiled. Playing it cool. "Okay," he said. "You're right. But I'm hungry, and the food here is *magnifico*. And frankly,"—he leaned in and lowered his voice—"even if it were the only way, it would still be worth going out on a date with you to eat here."

That came out sounding more objectionable than he had intended, but she didn't seem to mind. She giggled again, and blushed a little, too.

So Gail consented to having dinner with him, just dinner, no more. She didn't want to start something she couldn't finish.

Chapter Three

I first met Gail Bishop in an English Lit course I took as a freshman in college. She was one of the only good things college ever gave me. My friends and I were chatting about something or other, before class started, when I happened to glance up. From across the room entered a pretty brunette with a simple face and long, curly hair. She wore plain clothes—a T-shirt, jeans, and sneakers—and to most men, she probably would not have appeared incredibly attractive, but she transfixed my eyes. Quietly, she scanned the seating area, selected a lone desk along the edge opposite to me, and sat, placing her book on the desk before her.

Some friend had been speaking to me at the time, and I must have missed what he was saying, because he noticed my shift of attention. He asked, "Do you like her?"

"I don't know," I said. "I haven't met her yet."

"I have. She's in my psychology class. She wasted almost five minutes of the first class arguing with the professor. No one else could hear her. You know how it is in those lecture halls." He scoffed. "What a dork," he added.

I thought that was a pretty rotten thing to say. I had

not been there, and I didn't know what the disagreement was about, but if her psychology professor, I reasoned, allowed her to speak, and if he didn't kick her out of the class, then it must not have been that bad. For all I knew, she might have been the only one in class who actually *got* what the professor was talking about, and cared enough about it to say something.

"I'm going to go talk to her," I said.

I think he might have laughed at me behind my back, but I didn't care. I walked over and sat, backwards, at the desk in front of her. She was examining a map.

"Hi," I said, smiling.

She looked up. "Hi," she responded.

I introduced myself, but she didn't tell me her name.

"Can I help you with that?" I asked.

"I don't know. I was just trying to figure out how to get to my next class."

"Makes sense," I said. "So where is it?"

"STH 525"

She was clearly new, because that was one of the huge buildings that you couldn't miss, unless you simply didn't know what you were looking at. But then again, we were all new there, and I loved that I had the answer for her.

"That's the next building down from this one, just across Marsh Plaza." I pointed to an area on her map. "You know, with the Martin Luther King Jr. statue, with the flying birds, there. By the way, the seal on the ground, next to the statue? Don't step on it."

"Why not?"

"Because if you do, then you won't graduate on time."
That was the superstition, anyhow.

She looked sideways at me.

"Well, that's what they say," I said, apparently in a
way that brought a smile to her face. She had a wonderful
smile, and my heart thumped so, that I thought it was
going to come out of my chest.

"So we're here right now." I returned to the map. "You
go down, past Marsh Chapel, and then it's the building
right across on the other side."

"Oh," she said. "That's simple."

"Yeah. Pretty much. I had a class there yesterday. The
room numbers are a little funny in that building. I actually don't have anywhere to go after this class, so I can
help you find it."

"That's okay. You don't have to do that," she said.

I didn't know whether she was just trying to be polite
or whether she was pushing me off.

"I heard you had a blowout with your psych professor."
I changed the subject. "I didn't believe it, though, not
until I heard it from you."

"What?" She stared quizzically at me. Then she shook
her head. "It was nothing."

She paused.

"We just disagreed about what psychology was."

I chuckled at that, which prompted a dissertation on the subject. I don't remember what she said, but by the time she was done, I agreed with her point of view, and I knew in my gut that no one else knew what he was talking about.

———

"I've been running an SLP clinic in Worcester," Gail said.

The more things change, Eddie thought, the more they remain the same. She had moved to Worcester years ago to take an entry-level job in speech-language pathology. Eddie had not understood why that particular job was so important to her, but it was. And even though Eddie still felt a little sore that she had left him for her career, he was genuinely happy that she appeared to be succeeding in it.

The waiter placed before each of them a small plate on which sat three ravioli drizzled with a white sauce. Eddie looked at it and thought how lonely they looked, as though they were missing something: a carrot stick, a stalk of broccoli, a sprig of parsley... anything.

Gail took a bite, and groaned with delight. "Oh my God! These are delicious!"

But Eddie said, "I almost don't want to eat them."

"Why not?"

"They look... sad."

Gail almost laughed, but he seemed serious. She started feeling inexplicably guilty for biting into her own.

"What do you mean?"

"They're just sitting there on the plate, all by themselves, like there's supposed to be something there with them, like they've lost their better half."

Gail didn't know what to make of this conversation, but Eddie had a solution. He took a roll from the basket on the table, broke it, dipped one half in olive oil, and placed it in the empty space on his plate.

"There," he said. "That's better."

By now, Gail was holding in a guffaw.

He took a bite of ravioli. "So are you visiting Ann, then? How do you know Ann, anyhow?"

"Ann is my new business partner," Gail said, between make-believe coughs, which allowed her to cover her mouth so that he wouldn't notice her giggling at him.

"And you let her set you up on a blind date?" Incredulous.

Gail laughed openly now, partly from George's comment, partly because she was still holding one in from the ravioli discussion. "It was the only way to get her off my back."

"I believe that. So *you* are the old college chum of Ann's? How come I never met her when you were in college?"

Gail's countenance fell a little, because Ann had become her friend just as George had begun slipping away from her. "Well," she said, "you and I weren't talking very much back then."

"So you're doing well, then?" Trying to lift the conversation again. "You feel good about it?" He took a sip of Pinot Grigio and savored its tangy aromas.

Gail nodded. "What have you been doing? Last I knew, you were still working at... McDonald's? I think?"

"I got into real estate during the bubble, made a little money. I'm doing okay."

"So the way the market is... You probably don't want to talk about it, huh?"

Eddie smiled. "It's okay. I don't sell nearly as many houses as I used to. Back in the day, my phone was literally ringing off the hook. I would get buyers calling while I was on another call, wanting to plop down obscene amounts of money on houses that weren't worth a fraction of that, and I was coaching them on how to wine and dine the sellers, because they were desperate, and the competition was fierce.

"Now,"—he pulled his cell phone from his pocket and placed it on the table—"look at it, sitting all lonely there."

Gail had to admit, it looked a little pitiful.

"So, yeah," he continued, "I'm seeing a lot less business than I was, but I'm doing all right. I have some money saved, and the market looks like it's turning around. That's just the ups and downs of the market, you know?"

The truth was more grim than he let on. When the bubble burst and the crash hit, Eddie had kept up his extravagant lifestyle. Yes, he had saved some money during the boom years, but he had been burning through his savings, and now he was beginning to worry about making ends meet.

"Anyhow, my friends in real estate, they're the ones who started calling me 'Eddie,' because they said 'George' doesn't match my personality, something about it being 'too stuffy.' I don't see the difference myself. But I guess it stuck, anyhow."

"That's going to take some getting used to," Gail admitted. She still thought of him as "George."

It comforted Eddie that Gail still thought of him, or at least that she still thought something about him, even something as insignificant as what his name ought to be.

He smiled, as he always did, and said, tenderly, "I'd love for you to call me 'George.'"

———

After a scrumptious dinner, he sharing her sautéed white-fish, she sharing his stuffed pork tenderloin; and after cappuccino and a long, involved cheesecake discussion that resulted in them eating gelato instead; and after lots of reminiscing about the good times; and after the wine had worn off, Eddie found himself holding the door for her as she exited.

He didn't want to hold the door, because he didn't want her to exit, because he didn't want the evening to end. He didn't expect anything to happen between them, but he enjoyed her company. She opened in his heart a long-empty cavity, and filled it. Just sitting with her, talking to her, watching her, laughing with her, human contact with her filled that void. And he knew that as soon as she walked away, it would be empty again. And he would again need to close the lid on his heart, in order to keep the emptiness from leaking into the rest of his life.

He escorted her in silence down Watertown street, as the evening cars thunk-thunk-thunked down the old, concrete-block roadway. As she approached her car, Eddie saw its lights flash, a light-colored Subaru, the street-lamps reflecting off its trunk, its horn emitting a bleep of finality, and he felt the inevitable slipping-away of the evening coming upon him.

He walked around the driver's side and opened the door for her, turned to admire her before saying good-night. Bizarre, he thought, that he just now noticed, as the evening was coming to a close, the gorgeous green dress she was wearing, now shimmering in the night lights; her figure, flowing from her arms, down sleek legs, to a point at her toes. Tall and sexy and hadn't aged a day.

"You look good," he said. "Did I mention how good you look?"

"Is this about the cheesecake again?" she joshed.

"No," he said with bittersweet warmth. "It was just—Really good to see you again. I'm sorry we didn't do this sooner."

"Yeah," she agreed. "Me too."

For a moment, she forgot the reasons they hadn't done it sooner, and why she wouldn't have come even tonight, if she had been given the choice.

He brushed her hair back on the side and leaned in for a peck on the cheek. But she turned her head, and it landed on her lips.

She hadn't thought about what she was doing. Her head just shifted, of its own accord, and what was supposed to be a goodbye kiss between friends morphed suddenly but oh so naturally into an intoxicating gesture that stole her out of herself. She knew some reason why she shouldn't be doing this, but for the moment, she had forgotten what it was.

His hands caressed her face, his fingers pulling gently through her hair. As his lips met hers, she found herself being drawn into them, smooth as velvet, soft and supple. A wave of emotion passed through her and then receded, taking her strength with it, as he sucked the life out of her and into himself. She wrapped her arms around his torso, breathed in, tried to grab back what he had taken, a futile effort. Her legs collapsed from underneath her, and she fell against the car, his body falling over her in comfort and closeness.

He pushed off the car, away from her. Breathed for a moment. Then said, "I'm sorry. I didn't mean to do that."

That was all he could utter, and Gail also found her voice had left her. She nodded, sat behind the steering wheel. He closed the door behind her, and before her head cleared, he had left.

Chapter Four

I probably would never have even dated George, but then he kissed me. During my freshman year at BU, we took a literature course together. He somehow finagled his way into working with me on a poetry assignment. I don't remember how he managed that. We met in a study room during a free period.

He was reading Lord Byron:

> She walks in beauty, like the night
>
> Of cloudless climes and starry skies;
>
> And all that's best of dark and bright
>
> Meet in her aspect and her eyes.

We were supposed to be analyzing the imagery and metaphor. But I felt as though he were reading it to me, about me. He was cute and nice and sweet, but I didn't really know how to interpret him. The whole idea even felt weird. Classes and studies, they made sense to me. Romance, that was just something *other* girls read about in teen magazines or daydreamed about, and something old women tried to recapture in trashy romance novels.

Somewhere between "The smiles that win, the tints that glow" and "tell of days in goodness spent," while I was daydreaming—and maybe blushing a little—he leaned over and kissed me.

It felt like electricity flowing through my body.

Then he pulled back and just stared at me, as though I had drooled all over my front or something.

"What?" I said.

"Nothing. I was just wondering... Maybe we should get back to the assignment," he said.

And so we did.

It wasn't until a week or two later that he caught me before class and said, "I like you, you know."

"Well, I like you too."

"No," he said. "I mean, I really like you. I think you're the prettiest girl I've ever met— I sound like such a dork."

It didn't sound dorky to me. It sounded sweet. But I giggled, and he turned away.

"No," I said, "please don't."

I felt my face flush, and I was smiling from ear to ear. I remember the look on his face, a look that could only be caused by bliss, as if I had just made his day.

I don't know whether boys realize how funny that makes a girl feel, the first time she realizes that someone's falling for her. It's as if God never intended us to have that kind of power, to take on the responsibility for someone else's feelings.

Not to have any control over whether we'll make him happy or whether we'll devastate him, ultimately it's like having one's finger on the atomic-war button. Who can stand that sort of responsibility foisted on them?

But I was not thinking of those implications at the time. I was only thinking that yes, I liked him, too, and I was glad he was talking to me about it.

———

Eddie jumped at his cell phone, answering it even before he knew who it was. He had been doing so ever since the real-estate bust, because it could be a potential client calling, and he was desperate to be available, maybe a little too desperate. He was running out of money, fast, and other sources of income—including mooching off his parents—were scant.

He didn't feel right about mooching off of anyone, anyhow, especially not his parents. He loved to be generous with what he had. But while he could dish it out, he couldn't take it, because he feared that accepting charity made him less of a person.

He was also still reeling from the previous evening. He had never expected to have kissed Gail Bishop ever again. She might have been a name on a "celebrities I'd like to sleep with" list. But that was the closest he'd ever expected to get to her again. And now— What did it mean?

Gail was so difficult to read sometimes, one of her characteristics that excited him. The other was her passion, whenever she set her mind to anything, either boiling hot or as dense as ice, and nothing in between.

Whether or not the ice thawed, for the time being, he felt young again.

He pushed the green button on his phone without looking at the caller ID. "Eddie Chase," he said into the microphone.

"Eddie, Bob here," came the voice from the other side. "Ann wants me to ease into a conversation about your date last night, so that I can give her a scouting report. Oh, and I wasn't supposed to tell you that."

"Got it," Eddie said with a grin. "Well, you'll never believe this. Gail and I were married once, a long time ago."

"That'll teach you to go out on blind dates. Maybe it'll teach Ann a lesson, too."

"No, it was pretty good. It was nice to catch up."

"I didn't even know you had ever been married," Bob said.

"Yeah, well, it usually doesn't come up." Truthfully, Eddie didn't like to talk about it, because memories of Gail brought up bad feelings.

And even riding high on endorphins, as he was now, he wasn't ready to talk about the kiss, not even to find out how Gail felt about it.

Bob didn't push the subject. He respected Eddie's limits.

Eddie also had a silly, niggling fear that whatever he said might get back to Ann, and thereby to Gail, and the whole thing would blow up in his face, destroying whatever amicability he and Gail had built last night, and perhaps even destroying the friendships he had built with Bob and with Ann. Better just to let the whole thing blow over, or to let Gail say something, if she thought something needed to be said.

So he let the matter drop.

———

Gail's voice hooked me, something about its tone, its cadence. It hooked me and reeled me in. A woman of few words, but oh did those words pluck the strings of my heart. When she talked about her dreams, she seemed to be able to see into the future, to what she wanted, and just by telling you about it, she made it a reality, and you wanted it, too.

And want it I did. But instead of diving in and pursuing her dreams with her, I let her pursue them alone.

Our relationship started to go downhill when I walked in on her while she was studying in our bedroom. I told her how beautiful she looked, and how I wanted to take her out and wine her and dine her, how all of our friends would be envious of me, because I was married to the most beautiful, most exciting woman on the planet.

I remembered when words like that would have made her blush, or even swoon. But she was deeply engrossed in some -ology or another. She hardly even noticed me.

She was studying for her master's degree, and having a tough time at it— I knew that. I was working full time as an assistant GM at a McDonald's nearby. We barely made ends meet, between rent, food, and school bills, so we probably shouldn't have been dining out, anyhow.

But a woman can make a man feel bigger than the world with a simple smile. Or she can make him feel smaller than an ant with an accidental cold shoulder.

So instead of seeking to become involved in her world, in order to draw her closer to me, I backed off, because I didn't want to get hurt.

In the end, we were little more than roommates, living in the same apartment, occasionally sleeping together, almost never living the same life.

I'm not bitter. I mention it to point out my own sins. Because while she studied, I partied with friends. I ate and drank. Instead, if I had cooked something simple at home, or sat down and read a book in the same room as she, if I had just been around, maybe things would have been different.

Once, I pressed the issue. I wanted her to spend time with me and our friends, to take a break, to socialize. We ended up in a heated discussion, which she might not have called a fight, but I did. But I didn't want to fight with her. I wanted to support her. So I stopped pressing the issue.

I wanted to make her happy. But I achieved the

opposite. And some mistakes you live to regret.

Chapter Five

*G*ail sat across from little Evan, 8 years old, and his
mother.

"How do you feel about your stuttering?"

"I w-w-wish," the boy answered, "I c- could stop." With
each word he winced.

Gail nodded. She knew there was probably nothing she
could do to eliminate his stuttering, only to make it easier
for him to communicate with others. But she didn't want
to say so just yet.

"My little brother talked differently than everyone
else, too," she said. "Did you know that?"

Her brother Graham, several years her junior, was
born with a cleft palate. Even after surgery and speech
therapy and more surgery and more therapy, he still
spoke with a noticeable lisp. Eventually, he overcame his
problem completely, unlike what Evan could expect. But
Graham's life as a boy resembled Evan's.

"Did you m- make f-f-fun of him?" Evan asked.

She shook her head. As a child, Gail had accepted
Graham and loved him, because he was her brother, not
realizing at the time that this was the best thing she
could have done. But she had been wondering to what

extent teasing was an issue for Evan.

"No," Gail said, "but other kids did. Is there anyone who teases you about the way you talk?"

Evan shrugged his shoulders.

Gail wondered whether he had any siblings and whether they teased him for his stuttering.

"Well, I love my brother very much," Gail said. "And you know what he said once?"

Evan shook his head.

"He said, 'This is just the way that I talk. I can't help it.'"

Evan gazed up at her with rapt attention. She glanced at his mother, neither smiling nor frowning, neither urging her on nor panicked for her to stop.

Gail continued. "Now, not all the kids stopped teasing him. But some of them did. And the important thing is that he was happy, and he had friends, even though he didn't talk like everyone else."

Gail needed to talk to Evan's mother. Gail needed to tell her that Evan probably would never stop stuttering completely, and explain to her what she and other adults should do to help him lead a normal childhood regardless. She also wanted to talk about teasing at school and with Evan's siblings. Gail turned to her, but before she could say anything, Evan intervened.

"So..." he began, still deep in thought. "Didn' it h-hurt his — feelings when the k-ids t-t-t- teased him?"

Yes, of course it had. And it had caused Graham to shut down. He had entered high school before he finally discovered the self-esteem he needed to respect himself and his accomplishments. His story, in fact, inspired Gail to study psychology, and then to go into speech-language pathology, because she wanted to help kids who were facing similar challenges.

But Evan's question opened up the door Gail had been looking for. The two of them discussed the topic in some depth, and finally his mother did begin to smile. Evan's older brother did occasionally tease him about his stuttering, and Gail gave his mother some suggestions for how to deal with that situation. His classmates also mocked and derided him at school, which was interfering with his performance in class.

Gail suggested, "What if I arranged with your teacher to come to your school and talk to the class about stuttering?" She turned to Evan's mother. "Frequently, the biggest problem is that the other kids are ignorant. And sometimes, even the teachers. And once they see and understand what Evan is dealing with, they become a lot more sympathetic. That can remove a lot of the stress so that he can deal with the other issues more effectively."

After they had finished, Gail ran across Ann in the main office area and said, "That kid's going to be alright."

"Is that the only reason you're happy?" Ann said. "Or is there something more to it?"

Gail didn't know what Ann was talking about.

Ann must have noticed Gail's puzzled look, because she clarified. "How was your date last night?"

"Oh," Gail said. She had not really had a chance to talk to Ann yet, because they had been going nonstop since they got into the office that morning.

"The date was a non-starter," she said. And then, before Ann could say anything, "Do you know who that guy was you set me up with?"

Ann looked confused. "Eddie Chase? He's a friend, someone we've known for years. A nice guy, a little flighty, but nice."

"He's my ex-husband!"

"No!" Ann said, eyes wide. And then, with all seriousness, "No way. You were married to Juh— something, began with a 'J,' or a 'G'..."

"George Edward Chase."

"Oh God!" Ann covered her mouth with her hands. "I'm so sorry," in that melodramatic cadence girls sometimes use to indicate sincerity and urgency.

Gail wanted to put her friend at ease. "It's okay. We caught up, had a good time. And then..."

After a few beats, Ann apparently couldn't stand the silence anymore. "And then... What?"

Gail told her the story of the kiss, how George opened the door for her, how he made her feel special, how he was going to give her a peck on the cheek, how she turned and kissed him on the lips, how she wanted to feel him, to taste him again, how it turned out to be much more than either of them had expected, how she would have kept going, had not one of them regained his senses, and how she feared what would have happened if they had taken it farther. How he apologized and left without another word.

Ann listened intently, only interrupting to urge more details out of her friend.

Gail shook her head in dismay. By this time, she had sat down, and was feeling a little ill.

"I never expected that to happen," Gail said.

"Well, yeah," Ann answered. "So, what are you going to do?"

"I don't know. I don't know how I really feel about it. I feel funny. Confused. Not love, though. But he's always made me feel a little funny."

"Sounds like love to me," Ann said.

Gail didn't want to hear that. "We had some good food and wine. That was it; the alcohol. It was fun to catch up with an old friend, and I was probably still a little tipsy. Why do we have to make more of it than it is?"

"Because you nearly sucked the guy's face off!"

"An accident."

"You 'accidentally' nearly sucked the guy's face off?" Ann used the air quotes around the word *accidentally*.

"Look, I don't know that he wants to start anything, and I certainly don't." Gail felt confident about that, now

that she had said it. "We ended up miserable and
divorced, because we just couldn't make a life together.
Why would I want to go into that again? I mean, yeah,
maybe it would be fun for awhile, but I'd always know
that..."

Gail remembered George's sad eyes, whenever they
had fought, or more often when they *didn't* fight. She
remembered when she told him she wanted a divorce. She
couldn't stand to put him through that again.

"I just can't do it, okay?"

———

George did excite me, like no one else had ever before, like
no one else has ever since. His vigor, an excitement about
him, it flowed from every pore. His love of life, his love for
me. He swept me off my feet and into a wedding dress.
But that's when things started going downhill.

A musician once told me that as soon as a band gets its
first recording contract, that's when the band breaks up.
Because they stop playing for love of the music, and they
start playing for the money. That's how it was for George
and me.

My college fund had all but run out by the time I got
my Bachelor's in Psychology, but I knew I needed my
master's. My parents were tapped out, since Dad had just
gotten laid off and my younger brother Graham was just
about ready to enter college himself, and any extra money
rightfully should help him. My folks had done their part,

and I had to take care of the rest.

So getting married seemed like a good idea at the time. That way, George and I could pool our resources. He had a full-time job, assistant GM at a McDonald's. Yeah, I know. It sounds like a joke. But it paid the bills and the rent, and he could put me through school. George had dropped out of BU, in order to find himself. So George said he could put me through school. And then after I finished school and got a job, and after he figured out what he wanted to do with his life, then I could help him.

But I ended up having more trouble with my school work than I had thought I would. And I had expected trouble, because I needed to make up certain under-graduate courses in order to earn my graduate degree. George was constantly interrupting me and badgering me, to get romantic, or to go out, or to socialize with him and his friends. We fought about that. When we were still just dating, I could escape into my dorm room or into the school library. He seemed to understand that I needed time to work on my studies. But after the wedding, it was as if he had no idea that I actually needed some proximity to the class materials.

One night, I was so tired, my eyes hurt. I had almost failed a test, and I was trying desperately to make up some lost ground in a course on diagnosing speech disorders. George came up to me and started petting me, which I guess I should have taken as a complement.

Instead, I lost it. "Not tonight." Anger and frustration. "I have a headache, and I have to learn this information."

"Take a night off," he said, and he sat down next to me.

I don't remember how exactly it happened, but I ended up shouting at him, "Get the *fudge* out of here!" (except that I didn't actually use the word *fudge*) and I threw a book at him.

He escaped into the other room of our tiny, third-floor apartment. I remember hearing the door slam, and I didn't see him again until the morning.

Before too long, we didn't even have the fights to keep us company. If he saw me studying after school, which was practically always, he would simply leave, without a word. I suppose I deserved that. After all, I had told him I needed to be alone. And I comforted myself by telling myself that it was all for a good cause, and it would all get better after I had gotten back on track and completed my degree.

After another year, I began to wonder whether he was having an affair. He certainly had enough time to do so. He could go over to her apartment, wherever that was, and do whatever he wanted with her, and I would be none the wiser.

Around that time, I met Ann, and we occasionally studied together. I told her about my fears, and I don't think I left her with a very good impression of my then-absentee husband. But I didn't think about it very much.

My heart ached at the prospect that my marriage was slipping out from under me, but I escaped by throwing myself into my books.

Finally, I graduated, and I passed my boards, and I was ready to start working full-time. George walked up to me one day, kissed me, and said we should start over again, make a brand new life together. He said he had already scoped out some property in Hull, a tiny seaside community on the other side of Boston. He said he wanted to be near the sea, and that the sea air would do us both a world of good.

What he didn't know was that I had just that day received an irresistible offer. One of my professors had apparently been impressed with my dedication and effort, and he put a personal word in with the owner of a clinic in Worcester, 40 miles in the other direction. It was exactly the opportunity I was looking for, the chance to work with families and children, in private practice. I had feared I would have to work at a public school or hospital for a while, until I gained enough experience to find a job in private practice, or to start my own clinic.

Unfortunately, there was no way I was going to commute from Hull to Worcester and back again every day.

And then I realized, like a lightbulb going off in my head, that I didn't really care if he went to Hull. I didn't care if he was having an affair. I didn't care about anything, except my new job. I didn't care if I had to pay him back cash for my master's degree, as part of the divorce settlement. Even if that were the case, it would be worth it. And that's what I told him.

Chapter Six

"*A*nn, what's this note on the Andersen account?" Gail asked.

Ann stepped over to Gail's computer, leaned in to look over her shoulder at the screen.

"Oh," she said, "I just gave them a discount, that's all."

Gail's gut tightened, because she knew they were going to confront each other. But outwardly, she remained calm, managerial, just as she had learned early in this sort of situation.

"Why did you give them a discount?"

"They couldn't afford our normal rate," Ann explained. "There was no way they were going to be able to pay it, so I arranged a special deal, so we could help their son."

The "special deal" Ann had arranged, Gail saw, was to charge even less than what it would cost in time and office expense. That was a generous and heart-filled thing to do, but Gail knew that the clinic was never going to survive if they gave away their core services at less than cost.

This knowledge didn't make Gail's next words any easier.

She turned her chair around to face her friend and

business partner, then insisted that Ann sit. She looked the other woman in the eye and as calmly and evenly as she could, she intoned: "We can't offer discounts like that, Ann. If we do, we'll go bankrupt. I'll honor the discount, this time. But in the future, you have to check with me first, okay?"

Ann stared at Gail, a look of bafflement mixed with grief. "We have the extra time, because we don't have enough clients yet. It's not like we're doing anything else."

"We're doing marketing," Gail said.

"But this *is* marketing," countered Ann. "They'll tell their friends about us, and that will get us more clients."

"More clients who can't pay?" Gail shot back.

There were other low-cost services in the area, Gail explained, for people who couldn't pay their rates. Some of these services were available for free right through the public schools. But Gail offered premium services to premium clients. That's how she was able to provide such high-quality, personalized attention to each client. And if they lowered their prices in order to attract business, they'd only attract the wrong kind of client.

"It would be different," she said, "if it were some limited special we were running, or a coupon we sent to specific, qualified prospects."

Ann sat quietly, and Gail couldn't really tell what she was thinking.

"Trust me," Gail concluded. "I've done this all before,

and I know what I'm talking about. Okay?"

Ann nodded, slowly. She apologized and said she understood. But Gail wondered whether she actually did.

———

Eddie strolled through the open house, scanning the interior as he went. Spacious foyer, all in white, with a long, rounded staircase ascending to the second floor; ornate stone fireplace and walnut mantel; new downstairs bathroom, done in powder blue; large closets; an enter-tainer's dining room and kitchen, with an extra-large sink and stovetop. He turned on the faucet, and water cool and crystal clear streamed from the swan's neck. Eddie had already examined the exterior, done in flawless beige siding, and it looked as good as what he was seeing in here. Everything was of good quality and seemed in good condition, and the house was set in a well groomed, quiet neighborhood. If the upstairs was as nice as the down-stairs, this was a dream house. Eddie wondered why the owners were getting rid of it.

He had worked hard for this account, even fibbing a little during the interview. He took a moment to remember when buyers were coming out of the wallpaper, his phone ringing off the hook, when he could afford to turn away clients because he was too busy, when he coached buyers on how to woo the seller into choosing *them* and accepting *their* outrageous offer. Those were the days he sold houses for fun, not for food. Now, he fibbed, said he knew all about buying houses like this one. Indeed, he had sold one or two in neighborhoods similar to this, and he had sold houses at the same asking price as this one... when asking prices had been $100,000 higher than they were now.

Eddie was tired of dealing always with prospects, never real sales, would-be buyers always dangling their potential commissions just out of his reach, like a treat dangled at the end of his nose goading him to do tricks. Or was it the fear of poverty that goaded him on?

The doorbell chimed with a calm, almost soothing sound that seemed to pass effortlessly through the entire house. He started back to the front door, where the broker was greeting Mr. and Mrs. Gillespie.

Eddie called to them, then to the broker, "Thanks Milo; I'll take it from here."

They were a middle-aged couple, probably looking for a larger home in which to continue raising the kids, or perhaps even to move the parents in.

He talked to them as he began walking them through the house, pointing out every last feature. Asked them about their jobs, whether they threw many parties—and included a choice anecdote or two from his own. Asked them about their parents, about their kids. This last evoked a cringe from Mrs. Gillespie and an annoyed "No kids" from her husband. Eddie stopped asking questions.

Instead, he continued gushing about the size of the

house, its prestige, all the things you could do in it... the size of the closets. He told them it was sure to disappear from the market in no time flat, but promised them he thought he could grab it for them for a song and a dance, and then he regretted saying that. But Mr. Gillespie looked sideways at him, and Eddie somehow knew he had blown it anyhow.

———

Most of my parties succeeded, smashingly. Some fizzled, and others flopped; those hurt. But I feared most of all that one of my parties would completely fall apart, because once, one did.

I had invited almost everyone I knew over for a grand summer cookout. And grand it was. We had two grills going, plenty of food and music, beer and soft drinks. This was after I had moved to the house next to the beach. The sun hung overhead in a cloudless sky that day, and we spent the whole afternoon eating, swimming, playing volleyball, or just stretching out on the beach and tanning. I think a couple people even broke out my Scrabble set and played a few games.

But nothing lasts forever, and some good things end sooner than others. One of my guests had apparently had a little too much to drink, and not enough to eat, and he began taunting another guest, in jest. And this other guest had apparently also had a little too much to drink, and not enough to eat.

With the speed of a jackrabbit, the jesting turned into angry shouting. I actually saw the two of them walking up toward the house, joking like friends one second, taking verbal pot-shots at each other the next. I suggested that they come inside, thinking that I could calm them down. Unfortunately, they followed my suggestion, which meant that when their verbal sparring match turned into a full-blown fistfight, it resulted in broken dishes and furniture, as well as bloody noses and loose teeth.

Soon after, rumors of violence began to spread among the guests, and many of them began to pack up. When I saw this, I began to panic. I even heard talk of getting out before the cops showed up. They never did, by the way. But that didn't stop the bulk of my guests from deserting without even saying goodbye. And I felt powerless to stop it.

So when my sloshed street fighters started up again, I lost my temper. I yelled at them, told them that if they couldn't calm down long enough for me to call them a cab, then I would kick them out, and they could walk, and I wouldn't lift a finger to help them. It wasn't true, I'm sure, and it sounds pretty lame when I tell the story now. But at the time, I wasn't thinking clearly.

A few of my friends had stayed behind to help me sort through and clean up the mess. I am forever indebted to them.

One, while he was leaving, remarked, "You throw a

great party!" He might have meant it as a genuine complement—indeed that party had ended extraordinarily. But I
took it as a rib, which made me feel like crap.

I spent the next weeks contacting everyone on the
guest list, patching up relationships as best I could. For
me, it had not been a "great" party.

———

Gail managed to forget about George and his kiss, until
he showed up at the clinic several weeks later.

Alarmed, she asked what he was doing there.

"Ann invited me," he said. "I'm meeting her and Bob
here. We're going out for dinner."

"You're welcome to come, too," he added.

Part of Gail wanted to go along, but another part knew
she shouldn't. She shook her head. "No, I have a lot of
paperwork to do." A partial truth, but she could have put
off the paperwork until tomorrow, if she wanted to.

She changed the subject. "So how have you been?"

"Real estate sucks," he said, a little acerbically.

"Things not going well?"

"Eh. They'll turn around soon enough." He tried to
keep a positive outlook, but he was no longer smiling.

At that moment, the suite door jiggled, and Bob
entered.

"Hey Bob!" Eddie said, patting him on the back. "Hope
you had a better day than me."

"Yeah, well, a day's a day," came the reply. "Where's

Ann?"

Gail answered. "She's still with a client," motioning toward the session room door. "She should be finished soon."

Bob nodded. "Do you know if she called the babysitter?" His tone grated on Eddie's ears like finger-nails on a chalkboard.

"She mentioned it earlier," Gail said. "But I don't know if she got around to it."

Eddie knew that something awful must have happened that day to upset Bob. When Eddie's life felt out of control, he called on Bob for encouragement, because Bob kept his head cool while all around everyone was losing theirs.

Bob asked Gail how the business was going.

"Pretty well, all things considered. It's a lot of work, but I love it." As soon as the words left her mouth, she felt uneasy saying that in front of George, even though it was true. She knew he was fighting hard times; maybe that explained her reluctance. Or maybe she just didn't feel comfortable sharing her life with him, because they had not discussed the kiss, and it was still officially hanging over them.

Eddie glanced back at Gail. She still shone beauty, he thought, even in such an everyday setting, during run-of-the-mill small-talk about nothing in particular. An instinctive, involuntary thought on Eddie's part. He had accepted that he would always love her, at least in part, even though he had decided not to tell Gail. She wouldn't understand, he reasoned, because of their past. Best to stay at arm's length, to remain friends. And she would make a wonderful friend.

"George was telling me a little about the real-estate business," Gail said to Bob.

Bob set his teeth.

"Sounds frustrating," she said. "I hope things turn around soon."

"Not likely," Bob said. "It pisses me off." Then his expression changed to one of troubled thoughtfulness. "I've been noticing that lately. I'm angry. Why should I be angry?"

"Because you're probably trying everything you know how, and nothing's working."

Eddie realized that he was angry, too. "I've always tried to look on the bright side," he said, because this bright side, he felt, was the opposite of what he and Bob were feeling, frustration, anger, even envy at Gail. He felt envious of Gail, as though she had somehow stolen his success for herself. "I'm really glad that things are working out for you, though," he said.

"It's natural to feel anger when things don't work out as you feel they should," Gail continued. "It's as if... reality is butting its nose into your business, into your space, and you want to force it out."

"What's that? The psychology degree talking?" Eddie joked.

"More like years of experience, being part of a failed business, and then one that worked, and hitting a lot of potholes along the way."

Chapter Seven

*A*nn came out, escorting a little boy, three or four years old, and his father. She introduced them to Bob and Eddie, but not before Gail greeted the little boy with "Hey, Jeremy!" and stooped down next to him. "Say, 'My cat barks at dogs!'"

Little Jeremy grinned wide and said, "No! My cat goes *meow*! Dogs go *bark*! You're silly!"

"Yes, I am silly!" Gail confirmed.

Whatever Jeremy's problem had been, his father seemed pleased by his progress, because he shook both Gail and Ann's hand enthusiastically before he left and wished them both luck.

Afterward, Ann explained that at one time Jeremy couldn't say that, because he would have pronounced it "dod" instead of "dog," and "tat" instead of "cat."

Eddie noticed Gail's pleasure, and he basked in it a moment. He had never realized how important helping these kids was to her. But now he saw it in her eyes, the way they beamed.

He said, "Wow. I've never seen you at work before. You guys are doing a good thing here."

"Thanks," said Ann. "Hey, you should invite Gail along

this Friday."

"Invite me along to what?" An instinctive response.

"Ann," Bob began. "Maybe—"

"We're all going up to Eddie's parent's cottage at Ardor Point for dinner on Friday. You should come. Have you ever met Eddie's parents?"

Gail had not seen Ed and Marcia Chase since before she and George had broken up. But they had always welcomed her and supported her in any way they could, despite the fact that she had married their son at a young age. She didn't know how they would react to seeing her again, though, and she didn't want any trouble.

"Oh, I don't know," she said. "Ardor Point? Where's that?"

"Maine," the other three said in unison.

"Jinx!" Ann shouted like a little girl. "Can't talk until I say your name 10 times!"

"Fine, then," Gail said, turning to Ann. "I'll talk to you. You're all traveling to Maine... for a dinner party?"

"Well, we're staying the weekend," Ann said. "Didn't I mention that?"

"No, I don't think you did." Gail sounded annoyed, which reflected her mood.

Ann had been trying to set Gail up since she got here. Ann had set her up with George on that blind date. Then when that fell through, she started going through every single man on the Eastern seaboard, one by one, despite her promise to the contrary. Ann had even tried to set her up with a client, the widowed father of one of Gail's kids. And now, a weekend in Maine? Gail smelled a rat, and it stunk.

Gail turned to George. "A setup," she said.

"You mean, she wants us both... uh..."

Gail nodded. "Yes, trapped together in a romantic cottage for the weekend."

Bob glared at his wife.

George merely chuckled, at first. He said to Gail, "Look, I'm not interested in a romantic weekend. It's just a friendly dinner Friday night—we do that sometimes— and then we vacation over the weekend. You're welcome to come. I'd like you to come. I think you'd have fun, and I think Mom and Dad would enjoy seeing you again."

His mention of "Mom and Dad" bathed Gail in love, comfort, serenity. She might even endure a romantic setup, for the chance of seeing them again.

"But," he said, "if you have so much work to do that you can't spare even one weekend— Actually..." He shifted gears. "You could bring your paperwork with you and do it in a relaxing seaside locale." He raised his eyebrows. "Might be nice for a change of pace?"

"Oh," Ann said with a dismissive wave, "she doesn't have any paperwork that can't wait until Monday."

Gail considered the possible outcomes for a moment. "Do you think," she said, quietly, hope in her voice, "that they would really like to see me?"

"Oh, yes," Eddie said. "I'm sure they would. We can even call them and ask. They'd be thrilled to hear from you. You should have seen their reaction when I told them you were back in town!" Eddie pulled his cell phone from his pocket and began to flip through its stored list of contacts.

"No, wait!" Gail said. She still hadn't thought through all the possibilities, and she wanted to be able to back out. She had not considered that George would have told them about their date, but he might have. She needed time to think through the implications. "Don't call them," she said, relaxing her face into as easy-going an expression as she could muster. "Let's surprise them." A ruse, but it gave her a few days to change her mind.

"Okay." The corners of his lips turned up slightly.

———

From that first conversation with Gail, I was hooked.

Then one day, Gail and I were studying a famous poem for English Lit, "She walks in beauty, like the night." I read it to her.

That poem meant something special to me, because of a story I heard when I was a young adolescent, first discovering the fairer sex.

As the story goes, a few boys were gathered around chewing the fat, when a girl approached. While she was still a ways off, one of the boys saw her and, overtaken at the sight of her, rose and spoke: "She walks in beauty, like the night of cloudless climes and starry skies." Laughter rustled through the group, and red-faced, the would-be Romeo recoiled back into his seat.

In our youth, our friends may outwardly discourage us from expressing our passions, but we feel them. And we should never admit shame for appreciating the beauty of a woman, no matter how silly or extreme our friends may think us.

This particular poem already reminded me of Gail. Or rather, Gail already reminded me of this poem, not just because of her beauty, and that it had overtaken me, but also because of her passion, and that it moved me.

And by the time I got into the second verse, "the nameless grace which waves in every raven tress or softly lightens o'er her face"... I was convinced the poet must have written this for me, about her.

I saw invitation, longing in her eyes, or in my imagination, the passion she had awakened in me. I decided I would risk kissing her, whatever the result, because the worst she could have done would be to reject me, and it would be better to be rejected by her than not to share with her how I felt at that moment.

In a blur, I leaned over and kissed her, gently, on the lips. I longed to make the moment last, in case it was the last moment of my life. She kissed me back, her lips forming to accept mine, her hair yielding beneath my

touch, her eyelash flicking on my cheek, and I had found
heaven.

————

During the three-hour drive up to Ardor Point, Gail read
and napped, and chatted with Ann from time to time.

Mostly, Gail worried about what would happen when
she saw George's folks. She played over every scenario in
her mind, from pleasant surprise to startling indifference,
from happy reunion to shock and terror. She wondered if
they had changed much in the years since she had last
seen them, or whether they would even recognize her.

Bob's taste in music left something to be desired; to
Gail, it sounded straight out of *The Beverly Hillbillies*. *Ann
must really love him,* Gail thought, *to put up with that.* She
reclined in the back seat, as much as she could in the
cramped space, and distracted her mind by scanning
through a stack of back-issues of *Advance* magazine. A
trade journal wouldn't include very much that Bob would
find interesting. Occasionally, however, Gail ran across an
article *she* found interesting, and she wasted no time in
reading it excitedly to Ann. Get back at Bob for the music,
and help her feel better—impending doom tends to drag a
person down otherwise.

Meanwhile, Ann interrupted Bob's driving repeatedly
to ask if she should call his parents to check up on the
kids. Bob always answered the same: the kids were fine,
and she knew the kids were fine.

Finally, he said, "Are you going to do this the whole weekend?" glancing over at her with a crinkle around his eye.

After two or three hours of this, Bob pulled off the highway, and some tens of minutes later was barreling down Ardor Road, which led them down a long, flat strip of land, a peninsula, no more than a couple thousand feet wide. Staring out the side window, Gail could make out the sea in the distance, in between the trees as they passed. Suddenly, Gail felt tiny, insignificant, fragile, as though being surrounded by the infinite sea exposed her to danger, like being perched on the wing of a jet as it soars above the infinite clouds.

She was beginning to worry again, even though she knew it would do no good. However they felt about her, whether they still loved her or whether they hated her, whatever the result, even if they kicked her out and made her sleep in the car, she was still going to see them again, because there was no turning back now.

The wrongness of the situation hung over her, to spend a weekend in her ex's parent's cottage, with her ex in the next bedroom. *Why did I even agree to come out here like this?* There must have been a reason, and a pretty good one.

Because I want to see them.

She both desired and loathed seeing George's parents again. She desired to see them, because she missed them. She loathed seeing them, because she feared what they

would say to her, because she had not faced them since
before they found out that she and George had split up.

While Gail and George were married, they both
consistently told his folks that everything was "all right,"
even while their relationship was drifting aimlessly and
falling apart. She never let on that anything was amiss.
At first, they hid their situation, because they thought all
marriages go through dry spells. Then they hid it, because
they didn't want to worry the rest of the family. She could
only imagine how they took the divorce, but she knew how
hard her own parents had taken the news. In between
their supportive phone calls, some part of her knew that
they blamed themselves for not being more available, for
not stepping in and doing something to keep Gail's
marriage together. She had never faced that from
George's parents, and she hoped she wouldn't have to.

Gail turned her gaze back to the road ahead of them. It
split into two one-lane private ways, each one-way, one
going out and the other coming in. Gail surmised that the
two must meet further on, before they ran out of room and
fell into the ocean. Bob continued for a ways down this
road, threaded between houses on either side. Gail
couldn't see the water anymore, until the road began to
turn. Then suddenly the view to her right revealed open
ocean through loosely packed trees. She suddenly felt
small and insecure again, as she stared off toward the
horizon.

Gail thought she saw a landmass off in the distance. "Is that an island?" she asked, pointing out the window.

"Another peninsula, I think," said Bob.

Somehow, that made Gail feel a little more secure, to see solid land dwelling within the great expanse of the sea.

Bob pulled the car up into a small driveway and turned off the engine. "We're here!" he announced.

———

My father walked me down the aisle on a Saturday. George was staring at me from his spot on the dais, and I swear I could see actual stars in his eyes. Or maybe the stars were merely shining through my eyes. Catching my first sight of him in his black tux, blue-grey vest and tie, I thought he was the most handsome man in the entire world. And at that moment, he probably was, too.

Despite all that would happen afterward between us, that day still was one of the happiest of my life.

Dad walked me to the front of the church. And when the minister asked, "Who gives this woman to be married to this man?" Dad announced, in a voice he usually reserves only for sporting events, "Her mother and I!" Then he kissed me on the cheek, and hugged me, and he took George's hand and gave it a hardy shake, and hugged him, too. Finally, he allowed George to escort me to the dais. I guess he deserved license, because he had scrimped and saved to give his only daughter a wedding to remember.

After the ceremony, we were waiting to take pictures, waiting for the photographer to figure out something or other that was bothering him about his camera. George's father took us aside, and he officially welcomed me to the family, "before the festivities really start, and we lose our chance," he said. Then he and Mom Chase hugged me, and I felt truly welcomed, that this ritual represented more than just a duty for their son, that they were expressing their own pride in me, as though I were their own daughter.

I later discovered that they had pitched in a significant amount of money toward the wedding. They had done so anonymously, asking my parents not to reveal that they had helped out. But my dad eventually told me anyhow, pledging me myself to keep their secret, even from George. And I'm proud to say that I have faithfully done so.

———

Gail inched her way down the walkway and partway up the stairs to the cottage, dragging a small suitcase behind her. The cottage looked to her more like a beach house, with its white siding and green trim. But, Bob had explained, it was uninsulated and so couldn't be used in the winter.

Bob opened the rickety screen door and knocked, with Ann behind him and Gail behind her. The front door

swung open and to Gail's increasing dread, at the
entrance appeared Ed Chase, George's father. He apparently didn't see Gail, not at first, because he didn't take
notice of her. But she noticed him. His hairline had been
receding when she knew him, and now he was almost
completely bald, his remaining hair greying quickly. This
somehow made his jovial countenance seem friendlier,
and made Gail want all the more for him to like her.

She froze, stopped breathing, stopped thinking. She
should have been able to hear what he was saying to Bob
and Ann, but her ears must have been malfunctioning,
because all she heard was the sea wind, the waves
lapping the shore behind her, a distant dog barking, and
the creaking of the screen door being jostled on its hinges.
Gail's head began to spin, but she stood still, did not even
sway.

Bob and Ann parted, and Mr. Chase shifted his gaze
toward Gail. His expression shifted, as though a light
switch had been turned on somewhere, and he beamed.
"Gail! Oh my God!" He rushed down the stairs as quickly
as his aging knees would allow, and he hugged her and
kissed her cheek.

Gail had been biting her lower lip, without even realizing it. Now, she tried to say hello, but no words came
out. The sudden attention was more than she could take,
and all she could do was to drop her bag—where it fell,
she didn't care—wrap her arms around him, and hang on

for dear life, as a tiny tear began to trickle from her left
eye, then her right.

Chapter Eight

Mrs. Chase provided Gail with a cooler reception than her husband had, polite, friendly, but not bubbling over. A small woman with dark-dyed hair, she had always been quieter than her husband. And like Gail, she didn't enjoy surprises. She liked things to be planned, expected, and Gail didn't know how much Eddie had told her, or whether he had told her anything about setting another place at the table. For all Gail knew, she may have been planning on only two guests instead of three.

Or maybe Mom Chase had never forgiven Gail for breaking up her only son's marriage.

At dinner, Gail had barely touched her steak when Mrs. Chase said, "So, Gail, I understand you and Ann are in business together now?"

The tone of the woman's voice made Gail feel as though she were being accused of something. Why ask her instead of Ann? Was this the start of a grilling? Something else she would come to regret about the weekend? Her head began to ache, a blunt, dull throb.

"How did you arrange that?" Mrs. Chase asked.

Gail looked to Ann with a pleading expression, hoping she would notice Gail's distress and bail her out of the impossible spot she was in. Fortunately, Ann did apparently notice, or she just really wanted to talk about the subject. Regardless, to Gail's relief, Ann began telling the story of how they'd been friends since college, how Gail had been looking to make a change, how she had business experience in private practice, how Ann had been looking to get back into working, now that her kids were a little older, and how everything else had fallen together. Throughout this story, the others interjected with their own questions or observations, and Ann fielded them all, allowing Gail to breathe easy.

"Now," said Dad Chase, back again to Gail, "I was wondering: Moving back here must have been harder than moving out there. I mean, didn't you leave friends behind, back in... Where did you live again?"

Gail finished chewing and swallowed. "Auburn," she answered.

He looked at her quizzically. "Where's that?"

"In the Worcester area."

"Oh, so that's not too far from Boston, then."

His easy-going, conversational manner put Gail at ease. He had passed on that part of his personality to his son, a part of him she always had admired.

"It's about an hour away," Gail explained, "longer than I'd like to commute. I turned over the operation there to my office manager, and I don't expect to be needed very often."

Eddie interjected, "But won't you miss the people there?"

Gail had never truly thought about how much she would miss the people there, especially Clarice, her office manager. They had all pitched in and bought her a big cake her last day, and toasted her with champaign. Naturally, Clarice had organized the surprise and pulled it off, all without letting Gail in on the secret. At the time, Gail had felt proud and a little embarrassed to be getting so much attention. But while she was sure they missed seeing her every day, she had been looking forward to what lay ahead, rather than back to what she had left behind. And that's where her mind had stood, unwaveringly until now.

Before Gail could answer, Eddie's mother put in her two cents.

"Don't worry, George," she said, "Gail has always handled life changes without too much sorrow. And Ann is a wonderful partner." She turned to glare at Gail.

Eddie shifted his eyes to his mother for a moment, wondering what she was up to. Then back to Gail in an attempt to offset his mother's unpleasant undertones and rescue the conversation. "In any case," he said, "it's a brave thing to do, and I'm proud of you, both of you," looking to Ann now as well, "and wish you the best of luck." Impromptu, he rose his glass, which was half-full with red wine, and made a toast: "To Gail and Ann, success and fortune!"

"Hear hear!" said Ed Senior, raising his own glass, which the others at the table then echoed.

Gail felt herself involuntarily smiling and blushing, both hating the attention and adoring it.

———

I was at the mall with a girl—Lori, I think her name was. We went to high school together, and we were shopping, as I recall, for Christmas. Not a date, just shopping. But I liked her, and she probably liked me, too. We were next up in line at the cash register when a girl who had gone through earlier rushed back into the store carrying a bracelet. She said she was sorry, but she had accidentally walked out of the store with that bracelet on her wrist and forgot to pay for it. She plopped down a 20-dollar bill.

The cashier turned tomato-red, like she was going to blow a fuse. And I think I saw steam hissing from her ears. She began to scold the girl with the bracelet, and her scolding quickly turned into shouting, and shouting into yelling.

The girl began to slink back, and looked as though she might cry.

Without even thinking, I got in the middle. "Look," I said to the cashier, "it was an accident, and she's trying to do the right thing. You're not doing anyone here any good by losing your temper."

I probably sounded like I was talking down to her, as

though she were three. She took offense and started to shout at me for butting in.

"I don't need this," the girl with the bracelet eked out, choked. And she took her 20 dollars and ran—or rather, speed-walked—as fast as she could out of the store. She was clearly trying her best not to make any more of a scene, despite her embarrassment and hurt feelings.

I was livid. I spat out the words at the cashier: "*I* don't need this, either!"

I turned to Lori. "Are you coming?"

She reluctantly left her merchandise on the counter and followed me out of the store.

I don't know what anyone else in the line thought, or whether anyone else walked out. My upset had blinded me to anything except the injustice I had just witnessed.

As I recall, Lori asked me to take her home. In the car, she asked me who the girl was. I naturally didn't know, just some unfortunate person who had been shopping that day. I had never seen her before. After I cooled off, I tried to make conversation with Lori, but she didn't seem very talkative. I also tried to apologize for making a scene, explaining that I just thought it was wrong what that cashier did. She agreed, but Lori and I never spent any more time together after that.

———

"Did you ever remarry?" Mrs. Chase asked Gail.

Gail shook her head. Staring at her food, "Not interested in getting married," she said, softly. The woman was accusing her again.

"You know," said Dad Chase, "you were a good influence on George."

"Really?" That statement fascinated Gail.

She glanced at George, who was grinning and shaking his head. But he let his father continue.

"Oh yes. Before he met you, in high school, what, he was kissing a different girl every other week."

"You're exaggerating," Eddie said playfully.

"Maybe a little, but there were a *lot* of girls."

This comment elicited a giggle from Gail.

"He couldn't stay with one person long enough to find anything. And now..."

"Are you saying I sleep around?" Eddie said with a twinkle.

"Hey, I don't want to know what you do behind closed doors!"

Everyone chuckled.

"All I'm saying," and he spoke to Gail, "it seems every time I hear about his exploits, it's another hot date with yet another woman."

Mixed feelings rippled through Gail's stomach. She had not really dated at all since they had broken up. She'd met a handful of men. Once or twice she went out, at Clarice's urging, but she wasn't interested in relationships, and she wasn't interested in sex for sex's sake. Her

work was her life and her passion. Even so, her ex's
exploits belittled her, as if he had recovered before she
had. Envy wrapped her, envy of these women, whom she
didn't know and would never meet. She didn't want to
hear any more stories about Eddie's exploits, at least not
right now.

"Now, I played the field a bit, too, when I was his age
—"

His wife jabbed him in the arm, and he turned to see
her teeth shining at him.

"Even so," he continued, winking at George, "I didn't
know there were that many women in the universe!"

Everyone was laughing now, except for Gail. But Eddie
noticed that Gail didn't seem to be enjoying herself and
changed the subject. And Gail saw him notice, and for a
moment, she realized how much he had cared for her,
even though it didn't work between them, and the good
that being with him had done for her. She couldn't have
put the thought into words. Maybe it wasn't even a
complete thought. But she felt happy that she had met
him.

———

Gail insisted on helping Eddie clean up after dinner. He
objected, as she knew he would, but she told him it would
really make her feel better. That loosened him up a little,
but he still beat her to all the hard parts. He had already
carried in the worst of dirty plates and was scrubbing

them in the sink by the time she realized what was going on.

To keep her occupied, he asked her to pull some plastic wrap over the leftovers and put them in the refrigerator.

She was only too happy to help out, because she felt obligated, having caused such a stir at dinner. "I hope your mom's not too upset that I came," she told him.

"I'm sorry about that," he said. "I don't think she means anything by it." He lied. Eddie's mother had never quite gotten over his divorce, and he knew that she blamed Gail at some level. But he thought that seeing Gail again might loosen her up, show her how happy they both were and how much better it was now for both of them.

Gail knew that he was covering something up, though, because Mrs. Chase had never acted like that before, all the years they were married. Gail didn't believe she had changed that much, and she suspected it had something to do with the divorce. And she told him as much.

Eddie nodded. "I don't know what's up," he said. "We don't really talk about the divorce. We've never really talked about it. In a way, our relationship—you and me— ended up distancing my mother just as it distanced you from me." He was drying a glass with a towel as he turned toward Gail, to the counter where she had placed the food to wrap. "Does that make any sense?" he asked.

Gail felt awful. "I didn't want to cause any trouble,"

she said. "It just wasn't working out between us."

Eddie was already nodding before she finished. "I know. It's not your fault, and I don't think even Mom blames you. I don't see how anyone could. And— Hey, I'm happy. And you're happy. And now we're friends. Right?"

Gail agreed.

"All is good with the world," he said, his voice uplifting and cheerful.

But it didn't really make Gail feel any better. "Maybe," she said. "But sometimes you do what you have to do, and sometimes people get caught in the middle. And it just doesn't get any easier. Sometimes life sucks. And I guess that's okay. It doesn't mean anyone's done anything wrong. It's just a little sad sometimes." And then she added, "If it comes up, let your mom know I still like her, okay?"

He set down his dishtowel and placed his hand on Gail's shoulder. "I miss having you around," he said. "Thanks for coming."

Chapter Nine

I always tried to be a good girl, completing all my chores and my homework, and doing them well. As soon as I got home from school each day, I would get right to work. My parents rarely pressured me. Rather, I pressured them. My friends sometimes called on me while I was working, and I would say to my parents, "Tell them to stop bothering me! Tell them I'm doing my homework, and I'll come outside when I'm done!"

Even so, occasionally I did skimp or procrastinate on work that I disliked. Whenever it was my turn to collect and take out the trash, for example. I usually just barreled through, mumbling and grumping all until it was done. But sometimes the situation was more complicated than that. One day when I was eight years old, it had turned out especially bad for me at school. I don't remember what had upset me so, but I was upset, and tired. And it was my day to do the trash, the worst day of my life, I thought, in that kind of childish funk that turns the problems of the moment into an insurmountable fortress.

I collapsed on the living room floor and asked my mother, "Could you do it for me?"

"No," she said, "I'm making dinner, and I need you to take out the trash. Come on; it's not such a big deal. Just do it and it'll be done."

Instead of doing it, I continued to lay on the floor. I ignored one warning, two warnings, three... Until my father told me to go to my room, which I did willingly.

After a while, I grew hungry, and whatever Mom was cooking smelled awful good. I came down for dinner and found that everyone had just about finished eating.

Dad said, "Get back to your room. There's nothing here for you."

I was livid. You mean he was actually sending me to bed without any supper? Just like in the fairy tales? Yes, he was.

"He who does not work, neither shall he eat," he said. And over my childhood, I heard this repeated numerous times, though usually at my brother rather than me. I think it was supposed to be a quote from Shakespeare or the Bible or something.

My brother, he frequently butted heads with them, especially after he hit his teenage years. He once even got into a fistfight with my father.

Me, I took the lesson to heart and learned the discipline to follow through on what I needed to do, no matter how unpleasant. As a result, once I decided I needed something, I would keep at it with a single-minded focus, until I arrived. I rarely gave up. That's why, when I

decided to go for my master's in speech-language pathology, I threw myself into it, even if it meant I couldn't
maintain a marriage at the same time. And indeed, that
was the end result.

———

The next morning, Eddie guided Gail on a tour of Ardor
Point. He started by walking her down East Ardor Road,
on which his parents' cottage stood, toward the tip of the
peninsula, "the point," where it joined with Central Ave.

Gail had pulled her hair back into a ponytail, to keep
the wind from turning her curled locks into a tangled
mess. The salty air blew over her face, filled her lungs,
cooled her cheek, freshly hot in the mid-morning sun.

Even before they had left Eddie's front yard, she
started by asking him about the land mass across the sea.

"That's Birch Island," he said. "And the water here is
Ardor Bay."

Eddie knew all the residents of the neighborhood. Mr.
and Mrs. Maxwell, one house back up the road, showed up
for only a week or two in the summer, but their family
used their cottage every weekend throughout the
summer. Similarly, the Baldwin family rented out their
place to tenants at various times during the season, when
they weren't using it. Numerous others did the same.
Each year, Ardor Point was home to a constant stream of
visitors, some of them new faces.

Then there were Miss Houston and Mr. Keller, who

owned adjoining cottages along Central Ave. Both single and independently wealthy, they had consistently visited every weekend during the summer over the past three years.

"We're still trying to figure out what's going on with them," Eddie said. "I don't think we ever will."

Gail listened with fascination.

"We rarely see either one of them. Each most stays holed up in his cottage. But every time they meet each other in the street, as far as we can tell, they flirt. I don't think either has even been seen visiting the other's cottage. Half of us think they're meeting on the sly between the sheets. The other half think they're just both 40-year-old virgins."

Gail giggled.

As they passed the cottage next to Eddie's, a voice called to them: "Hey! Whippersnapper!"

Eddie called back, "Hey yourself, Old Man!" Then to Gail, "Come on, let me introduce you."

They climbed several steps, up to the front yard where an elderly couple, both with snow-white hair, were reclining in lawn chairs overlooking the bay. From here, Gail could also make out sail- and motorboats in the distance, which cut the sea as they plowed through it.

The old man eyed Gail up and down through thick glasses—which made her feel a little uncomfortable—and winked at Eddie. "Who's the lovely, lady you're escorting today?" He spoke in quick, short starts that chopped up his sentences in awkward fragments.

The woman rolled her eyes.

"Uh, no," Eddie said. "Gail is just a friend."

The man seemed surprised. "I didn't know you had, any friends who were girls."

The woman intervened. "Now, Frank," she scolded him, evenly, firmly. Then to Gail, "I think it's wonderful that George has taken up friendship with a fine young woman. Much better than the parade of bodies he usually keeps company with. Here, pull over that chair," motioning to a nearby lawn chair, "and sit with us a while."

Gail obliged, because she liked the old woman and wanted to meet her, and also because she was perversely curious to hear more about the "parade of bodies." Apparently, a good sleep had quelled the revulsion she had felt at the subject the previous night.

Eddie, on the other hand, couldn't believe his ears. True, he had not taken many female friends—or *any* for that matter. But this was a side of Mrs. Porter he had never seen. He stood, uncharacteristically still and silent, nonplussed.

"Well," said Mr. Porter to Eddie, "are you going to sit too?"

"Right," Eddie said, and he grabbed a chair for himself.

"And," said Mrs. Porter, "since we haven't been properly introduced," glaring at Eddie—

"I'm sorry!" Eddie interrupted. "You're right." And he properly introduced Gail to Frank and Dolores Porter. They had been coming to Ardor Point for longer than Eddie knew.

"Twenty-five years," Mrs. Porter said.

"No," said her husband. "Twenty-four."

"It'll be 25 this September, when we came up that first year after our 30'th anniversary. And the weather turned cold, remember? We had to put a fire in the fireplace and huddle up around it just to stay warm?"

"Well, I meant, 24 *summers*."

"Sure you did."

A deaf man could have heard the sarcasm in her voice, but he was grinning at her ear to ear, a toothy, flirty grin, and for a moment Gail feared he might make a lewd gesture. Ironically, far from turning her off, this little scene charmed Gail, that they would still feel that way about each other after being married for so long, that true love did exist in the world, even though she had not seen it.

Doing the math, Gail asked, "You've been married 55 years?"

"Yup. Almost," Mr. Porter said.

"You were there during the Great Depression, weren't you?" Eddie said.

"I was *born* during the Great Depression. But too late

to remember it. I remember WW2, though."

Mrs. Porter nodded. "War was so much different then than it is today. Just in terms of popular perception."

"Yes," said her husband. "People cared about the war. You saw, full-page ads in the newspaper, or in magazines, to drum up support. Completely different than, the wars they have going on today."

"We made a lot of sacrifices for the war," Mrs. Porter explained, "so it was important for there to be popular support. There was a lot of media propaganda, and very little public dissent. My mother went to work in a factory, and my brother and I had to look out for ourselves after school. And rationing meant we couldn't get a lot of things we wanted." To her husband, "Do you remember that?"

He nodded. "We were always running out, of butter and sugar. We probably didn't, need that much anyhow." He chuckled. "My brother was, a little older than me, and ate, more than his fair share. I remember that. And we worried, if the war kept on, he might get drafted."

A lull in the conversation.

Gail was on the edge of her seat. "So?"

"So, what?" Mr. Porter asked.

"Did the war end in time?"

"Yep. I remember, my mother was, crying on V-J Day, and I didn't, understand why at the time. I thought it was, something bad, and didn't even ask. I didn't even ask, what the problem was. But it was because, you know, she was happy that Roy, didn't have to fight."

"Where are my manners?" said Mrs. Porter. "Would you two like something to drink? Some iced tea or lemonade?"

"Oh no, that's fine," said Eddie.

"Nonsense," said Mr. Porter. "That's a, prime idea Lola. Go make us, some iced tea okay?"

Gail felt a little guilty that Mr. Porter was pressuring his wife into serving them. But she understood why they were George's friends. He had always loved life, and stories of life, as they seemed to. That was one of the things that had first attracted her to him.

Gail decided to exercise her woman's prerogative. "I'll have some iced tea," she said to Mrs. Porter, "if you let me help."

"Fine idea," she said. "Let's go." She stood, and Gail saw, far from being the frail woman Gail thought she was, Mrs. Porter's small body was as robust as that of a woman half her age.

Inside the cottage, Gail and Mrs. Porter talked about Gail's job, her relationship to George ("an old friend of the family who had fallen out of touch"), her relationship to Ann, her experiences since college. Mrs. Porter insisted that Gail start calling her "Lola," and Gail obliged. Doing so felt awkward at first, like a new tooth that was coming in where an old one had fallen out, but she quickly got used to it.

Lola made Gail feel comfortable, like a maternal figure she could almost talk to. Her way disarmed Gail's defenses, because she reminded Gail of a mentor she had once had, wise and supportive, who had helped her through some tough times in her career. They had not always agreed, but Gail knew that her mentor always respected her unconditionally and had earned her respect in return.

Somewhere between a boiling kettle and tea in the teapot, Gail asked Lola, "Tell me more about the girls George sees."

The old woman stared back in amusement. "I thought you two were just friends."

"Well, we are," Gail said. "But I'm curious."

"You're friends, but you're wondering if you might become more?"

Gail didn't want to share their past, because it would just make relationships awkward, and she hoped that George would also be discrete about it. "No," she said. "Nothing like that. I don't think we have a future."

Lola pulled the tea bags from the teapot. "Ironically, I think someone like you would probably do a lot of good for him. I understand he was married once, before Frank and I met him. I imagine she could have been someone like you. But I guess it didn't work out."

"Why didn't it work out?" Gail's curiosity had won out over her apprehension at knowing what others thought of her behind her back.

"Not sure," Lola said, lifting a glass pitcher from a shelf. "They don't talk about it much. And even if they did, I don't much like to gossip. But ever since we've met George, he's been like a nephew to us, and his parents have been like brother and sister. I'd like to see him find a good woman. I think he'd be happier." She sighed. "Alas, it's probably not to be."

She pulled several ice-cube trays from the freezer. "Why don't you grab four glasses out of that cabinet there." She pointed.

Gail obliged, wondering why Lola would think that she had made George happy, all those years ago. He had not seemed happy to her. She remembered him being as miserable as she.

"But you asked about the girls he brings around," Lola said. "They're not the kind you should take home to mother, if you know what I mean."

To hear her impressions confirmed so bluntly struck her funny bone, and Gail giggled nervously. "Yeah, I know," she said, choosing two tall glasses from the cabinet, with designs on two more. She placed them on the tray that Lola had previously set with spoons, sugar, napkins, and a cut lemon.

"Good looking girls, don't get me wrong," Lola continued. "And George is still a handsome, young man. But I think he goes for the kind of girl to whom looks are the only thing that matters. A few I honestly couldn't carry on a conversation with. Literally."

Gail guffawed, a reaction that evidently pleased Lola.

She waited for Gail to calm down. "That sort of thing is nothing to build a life on. Eventually, it passes, and then you realize that you have nothing left."

She sounded as though she were speaking from personal experience. But Gail didn't pry, not because she thought that Lola wanted to keep her story a secret, but because Gail didn't want to share her own story in return.

Gail wanted to hear more about George's "bodies," but by this time, the tea was ready, and all that was left was to bring it out to the men.

Chapter Ten

"*I* know what," said Eddie. "Tell her about how you two met."

"How we met?" Mr. Porter said. "We met in college like every, other couple in the 50's. Nothing special about that."

"Oh, you're such a romantic," his wife said, rolling her eyes again. "I was in my senior year—and back then, women went to college to find a husband, so I was running out of time. One day, I walked into the student union, wearing one of those pouffy, pleated skirts that all the girls used to wear back then. And some pervert—"

"That's me," Mr. Porter interjected.

"I feel someone's hand up my skirt!"

"Oh my God!" Gail said, aghast.

"It was an accident!" Mr. Porter said.

"Sure it was." His wife had that sarcastic tone in her voice again.

"Right. It was," he repeated.

"Hey," she shot back playfully, "you already had a chance to tell your version of the story. Now it's my turn."

He leered at her lasciviously, and Gail was almost afraid that they were going to start making out right

there on the cottage lawn, a thought both romantic and
disturbing at the same time.

"I twirled around ready to punch someone in the nose,"
she continued. "You see, I grew up in a house full of
brothers, and they used to invade my space to upset me,
when I was little. And so I learned at a young age to
defend myself. So I twirl around ready to fight. And you
know what those pleated skirts do when you twirl in
them."

"Oh no!" said Gail.

"And so here I am with some guy's hand up my skirt,
and everyone in the room is getting an eye-full." Her face
turned red, as was Gail's, but she continued on. "It all
happened so fast. I hit him upside the head, as hard as I
could, which fortunately wasn't too hard, but I knocked off
his glasses in the process. Meanwhile, he had been sitting
at one of the tables there, and I guess he had been
stretching or something—"

"I told you it was an accident," he said.

"— and I wasn't watching where I was going, and I
ended up running right into him. So there he is with his
glasses on the floor, and he can't see without them, but he
realizes something's gone wrong. And I look, and his face
has turned red as a beet. And everyone in the room is
staring at us..."

"Good times," he added.

Gail picked her jaw up off the ground. "So then what

happened?"

"I asked her to marry me, is what happened," he said.

"And you've been blissfully happy ever since," Gail said, more a question than a statement, though everything she saw showed that they knew who they were, where they had come from, where they were going, and that they were doing it together.

"Actually," he said with a grin, "that whole story, we made it up."

Gail looked at Eddie, who was grinning, too.

Gail squinted in confusion, but Lola came to her rescue. "The truth is that if such a thing had happened, back then, we probably would have bought a heap of trouble, or at least a talking to. In some places, boys and girls weren't even supposed to be walking down the street holding hands. But Frank and I were always rebels, so one day, we made up the spicy version of how we met, and we agreed always to tell it instead of the real story."

Gail sighed in relief, feeling a little embarrassed for having been taking in like that.

"Don't worry about it," Eddie said. "I was fooled the first time I heard it, too."

"We weren't always happy after that, though," Lola said, looking at her husband, who was nodding. "But on balance, I think we were."

She returned to Gail. "After we were married, I went to work as a secretary to help put Frank the rest of the way through college. That was unpopular back then, for a wife to work outside the house, especially when her husband wasn't. I guess it's still unusual, but there doesn't seem to be so much prejudice about it now. After he graduated, he got a job on the executive track, and I quit my job, and we moved to the suburbs and started a family."

"That's when our problems really started," he joked.

But she nodded, in all seriousness, "Yes. When you're young, you think having kids is going to be the most wonderful thing in the world, especially back in the 1950's, when everyone was having a huge family. But in reality, it makes everything more complicated."

"And because of my job," he said, "I wasn't always— I worked long, hours, you know? That's what we, did back then."

She nodded. "Nowadays, fathers are expected to spend time with their children, but back then, it wasn't unusual for a professional man to be an absentee father. And then there was that time we thought you were going to be laid off."

He nodded. "Yep. That was in, years later, in '66 I think. *Almost* didn't make it." He radiated pride at the word *almost*.

Eddie had been sitting quietly, nodding at appropriate times, laughing at the appropriate times, but otherwise attentively listening. He loved hearing the Porters tell their stories, and he could listen to them over and over again. He also could tell that they enjoyed having an audience, and he endeavored to play the part of a good one.

Eddie now spoke. "You guys should go on the conference circuit. These stories deserve a wider audience."

"You're full of it," said Mr. Porter.

Eddie grinned. "Seriously, though, you tell your stories so well, and there are lessons in them that the younger generations need to hear."

Gail nodded, spontaneously. "I might get married again, if I could be guaranteed to be as happy as you two are." It was the kind of true love she had fantasized about when she was little. And she immediately regretted mentioning that she had been married at all. But nothing came of it; no one seemed to notice, or to care.

———

Gail stepped out of her sandals and savored the feeling of cool sand oozing between her toes. The beach was small, bordered by a large rock on one side, with seaweed where the sand met the sea, and with grass on a third side. She closed her eyes, let the breeze caress her neck, breathed it in. The smell of the sea always made her feel different, romantic, from the time she was a teenager. She had only visited the beach occasionally, usually with a boy. They would go out on summer evenings, when it was just warm enough that they didn't need to wear sweaters or jackets, bathing suits under their tee-shirts and shorts, and she would take off her sandals, and they would sit on the beach and make out.

She sighed.

And now she was standing here, on the beach, next to a man she had once found incredibly attractive— who she *still* found incredibly attractive. A man she had once cared deeply for. She opened her eyes, considered him. He was staring out into the sea. It was a shame that it didn't work out between them, because he had a tender heart and a good soul. But he was the kind who needed fun and excitement, whereas she needed vision and stability.

There was something about their marriage that she always wondered about, and recalling Lola's comments about Eddie's "bodies," it reminded her of it.

"Can I ask you something?" she asked.

"Of course, anything."

"When we were married, did you ever cheat on me?"

So blunt a question, it took Eddie by surprise. For a moment, his mind travelled back to a particularly lonely night during their marriage. But he had decided never talk about it, because he didn't see that it would help anything to discuss it now, or ever. He needed to find some way to deflect the conversation.

"What made you ask that?" he asked.

"I get the sense that maybe you did—" She corrected herself. "Back then, I got the sense that maybe you had."

Eddie put on a party face, a polite smile, almost fake.

Normally, a statement like that would come across as an accusation. But he didn't want to let his feelings of guilt make him seem guilty, and he didn't want to talk about it, didn't even want to think about it. It wouldn't have helped anything to talk about it back then, and it certainly wouldn't help now, after all these years. So he put on a friendly face to cover up his true thoughts.

"I would understand," she continued, "if you had. I know that I made you second place, and I'm sorry." She could hardly believe her ears, but she also felt she needed to say this. Some part of her had felt guilty for too long. "I'm sorry I put our relationship in second place." But saying it didn't make her feel less guilty.

Eddie remembered how he had felt about her, and acutely realized how strongly he felt about her now, how much he still loved her. There was some part of him that would always love her, no matter what. *And that's okay,* he thought, *even if nothing ever happens between us.*

Sudden, mournful longing.

He silently refused to answer her question about cheating. And now, another reason: he didn't want her to apologize for cheating on him, ever. Whether she had or hadn't, he didn't want to know. He would be happier believing that she hadn't.

So instead of answering her question, he revealed his own thoughts regarding whose fault it was. "I'm also sorry," he said, "for letting our marriage slip away. I mean, I knew your career was important to you. That was one of the things that I loved about you, from the very beginning. And I should have found ways to support you better, to be a part of your world and your goals, because they were important to you. Instead, I drew away and left you to fend for yourself, and that wasn't fair to you. If I had to do it over again..." And his voice trailed off, his stomach churning.

If he had to do it over... If only he could reset their relationship and try again... It was at that moment that he decided that even if he couldn't start over, he must try. Why must he try? Not because she was worth fighting for, even though she was. Not because this was something worth trying even if it failed, because he had not even thought of failure; failure was not an option. It was simply a truth he knew, something God must have revealed to him deep in his soul, that this was his destiny.

He collected himself and finished his sentence: "If I had to do it over again, I would make sure I was part of your life."

Gail didn't know what to make of that.

Chapter Eleven

*G*ail and I both worked hard. That's how she made it through her master's program, how she passed her boards, how she obtained her first job. It's how I managed to put dinner on the table of our third-floor, three-room apartment. And my hard work is also why they didn't kick her out of school for failing to pay her tuition.

I spent untold hours at the Mickey-D's on Commonwealth Ave, sorting through frozen french-fry orders and customer complaints, arranging employee work schedules, and picking up the slack for local slackers who also supposedly "worked" there. I don't mean to sound bitter about it, because really it was an enjoyable job. I met a lot of nice people, and not all the employees were slackers. But I knew I was destined for greater things, that this was just a stop along the way, until I figured out what road I wanted to take.

But Gail, she lived for her career, forsaking all others, keeping herself only for it. And I was happy to support my wife in her calling. I loved her for the passion she showed. She was going to go into private practice, and she was going to help untold hundreds of unfortunate kids who otherwise would daily be picked on for talking funny. It was sad and inspiring at the same time. And how could I but fall helplessly in love with her? How could I but sacrifice myself to help her reach that goal?

Yet, familiarity breeds contempt.

Night after night, I trudged home, after long hours spent jumping around like a Mexican bean in order to keep up with the fast food business, broken only by brief respites inhaling the aromas of the cheap food business. And I tried to snuggle up next to Gail on the couch, her nose in a book, and she told me I was disturbing her. Or I told her to take a break from her books and join me in a candlelit dinner, and she said, sorry, but she just didn't have the time. Once, she was studying in the bedroom, and I walked in stark naked and lay down next to her; she said I bounced the bed and made her lose her place. I was *this* close to meeting her at the door, dressed in nothing but Saran wrap.

One night, I told her to take a break and come out to dinner with some friends. I was tired of spending my nights alone, and I wanted to spend time with other people and with the woman I loved. I don't remember exactly what I said. I do remember, the more I pressed the issue, the more upset she became. I ended up leaving alone, dejected.

I stopped pressing the issue. I stopped arguing with her, because I didn't want to fight. Instead, when I saw her studying, I left quietly. I went out more and more frequently, to eat and drink with friends, or alone, and to try to distract myself from how I alone felt. Sometimes, I wouldn't even stop at home. I wouldn't call Gail. I would just stay out late, come in late, maybe give my wife a kiss before bed. She never objected, and for that, I was grateful, because it was better than fighting with her.

————

Gail and Eddie ambled back to the cottage quietly. Neither one could tell what the other was thinking, but both wondered.

George's last statement had hypnotized Gail: if he could start over.

If she could start over... That was a thought she had not considered. She didn't know what she would do. She had always done everything she needed to. It just didn't work out. She and George were not the right people in the right place at the right time to make it work.

For a moment, she wished that they could start over. But she knew they couldn't. Even if they were to try, the attempt would come to ruin. And that fact saddened her.

Was she destined to sadness? She had always believed that she could be happy, if she worked hard and achieved what she sought. She needed to talk to Ann, to sort through the confusion, penetrating itself into her heart. She always used to talk to Clarice, from as soon as she and Clarice were friends. Clarice wasn't here, but Ann was. And Ann was her friend and partner. She picked up

the pace, unconsciously, but noticeably enough that
George commented on it.

Meanwhile, Eddie strolled along, one foot on cloud
nine, one foot in hell. He had to find a way to win Gail
back. He would woo her, as he had before. he would
romance her. This time, he had the advantage, because he
already knew her. He began brainstorming ideas. Maybe
another romantic walk on the beach. Maybe a trip sailing,
on the water where two people can be alone together.
Maybe a special dinner— Or breakfast, a romantic breakfast as they used to have. And whatever was on her mind,
he would listen to her; he had always known how to
listen, when he had a mind to.

He glanced over at her, her face set, expressionless,
determined, maybe even upset. She quickened her pace.

"What's wrong?" Eddie asked.

"What?" she said, as if he had disturbed her deep
thoughts.

"You're walking faster. Is something wrong?"

"Sorry." Her eyes shone glassy. "I didn't realize."

"Anything I can help with?"

"No."

"Please? What's wrong?"

Gail didn't want to talk to George about her feelings,
not yet in any case. "Nothing's wrong," she said. "I was
just thinking."

"Oh." But he didn't believe her.

As they approached the cottage, Gail could hear Mrs. Chase talking in the living room.

"What made you decide to go into business for yourself?" she asked.

Ann explained that she never would have done it without Gail, because Gail had most of the business experience.

Mrs. Chase asked Ann what exactly she does in private practice that she couldn't do in a hospital or school.

George opened the front door. By the time he and Gail had made it to the living room, the door had swung closed with a loud bang.

Mrs. Chase turned in her easy chair, toward Gail, and said, "Ann was just telling me about her practice. It sounds like you two are doing some exciting things!" with a little too much enthusiasm.

What Mrs. Chase said didn't bother Gail so much as the tone in her voice as she said it, as though she meant to patronize Gail. She had been talking down to her all weekend, and Gail didn't know how to stop it. Furthermore, this was too much. Gail's business was her life, what she had worked for with unrelenting dedication for untold years, and she couldn't bear being demeaned in it.

"Neither of us could do it alone," Gail said, in an acerbic, bitter tone. "I wouldn't have done it without her, and she definitely couldn't have done it without me."

Ann jerked back in her seat, shocked.

"Okay, then," Mrs. Chase said, "I seem to have accidentally hit a sore spot. I'm sorry."

Gail did not believe that it was an accident. But what dismayed her was that this woman, who had once been so kind to her, was now acting so cruelly. Gail knew Mrs. Chase held an unfair grudge, because of George, and Gail needed to talk to her about it, get it out in the open so that they could deal with it. But before Gail could think of what she needed to say, Ann shot back.

"I don't want to be mean, but you'll have to excuse Gail. Sometimes, she gets so caught up in the cold, hard business facts that she forgets about the human equation."

"Better than going bankrupt," Gail said through clenched teeth.

"Puleeze! You learned from a woman who drove her own business into the ground."

"That's not fair!"

Joan Langley, Gail's first boss, wasn't even a speech-language pathologist. She had partnered with an SLP, however, and her clinic went down because of a string of bad luck and misunderstandings about the market, and also because she couldn't stand up to her partner. Gail couldn't do anything about bad luck, but she had studied hard, and she knew her business.

"And your own practice in Worcester is practically run by someone else."

Gail glared in amazement. That was a completely different situation. Gail herself had built that business from nothing. It was all her. Clarice had proven herself a competent office manager, and someone worthy to take up Gail's mantle.

"Face it," Ann said. "You couldn't make it without me."

That hurt. Maybe Ann spoke the truth, but only a partial truth, and she said it hurtfully. While Gail enjoyed the rush of entrepreneurship, even fed on it, she had no wish to go it alone. She had tried that once before, and experience had taught her that it's much better if you have someone to share the work, the challenges, the successes, and even the failures.

She stood, dumbfounded and betrayed. How could Ann have so quickly turned on her like that? They had been experiencing problems, true, but Ann had always been a faithful companion.

Eddie had been watching this firefight develop, with his own, flesh-and-blood mother in the middle. He did not notice at first the look of satisfaction, the sinister grin growing steadily on her face. As each salvo flew, he felt a greater and greater dread. At first, he denied there was really a problem; then, he hoped it would resolve itself; now, he was so grieved, he saw that he needed to get involved.

"Calm down, everybody," he said, stepping into the war zone.

"No need," Gail said, nose high in the air. "I'm perfectly calm." Even she didn't believe that.

Eddie heard the antagonism laced throughout her voice. "Good," he said soothingly. "Because there's nothing here worth getting worked up over."

"Oh sure," Ann said. "Take her side."

"I'm not taking sides," he said.

Gail knew that he had been Bob and Ann's friend much longer than he had been hers, not counting their disastrous marriage, which surely would not have counted in her favor. "And even if he did take sides," she said, "he wouldn't take *my* side."

"You think not, huh?" Ann was clearly mocking her. "Of *course* he would take your side! He's obviously in love with you."

"Hey! We're just friends!" Gail retorted.

This hurt Eddie more than if she had just blamed him.

"Right," Ann sang with contempt. "Romantic strolls down on the beach. Did you have sex right away, or decide to go back later, to do the deed under cover of night?"

Gail couldn't believe her ears. "Okay. That's out of line. Take that back."

Eddie felt helpless to stop what was coming.

Ann put on an air of indignation. "Why should I take it back, if it's the truth?"

Gail couldn't stand it any more. "I can't reason with you when you're like this," she said. And she stormed out, through the kitchen, and out the front door, slamming it on her way.

"Bitch!" Ann said, half under her breath. She crossed her arms and thumped back on the couch where she had been sitting.

Eddie glared at her, not believing what he had just witnessed. What had come over them? Eddie's mother, still observing quietly, also stared, a blank look on her face.

Ann took a second, then she stood. "It's not my fault," she said before climbing the stairs and marching to her bedroom.

Chapter Twelve

O ne lonely night, after a late night at work, I stopped by a familiar hangout—familiar for me, anyhow—a restaurant near to where we lived. Whether Gail was studying at home or had remained at school, I didn't know. And what she was doing, I didn't know.

I sat at the restaurant bar, I don't know how long, watching TV and nursing a vodka tonic. A woman walked up and ordered a drink. I noticed her, as I usually did any beautiful woman who entered my sphere of observation. She had dark hair, completely black (like Gail's), but straight, layered to just below her chin, and a square face with dark eyes and prominent eyebrows. She was a little older than I, but not by much, probably approaching her thirties. She sat a couple stools to my left and greeted me in a sultry voice, sending me a polite smile.

I returned the favor, as best I could.

She introduced herself as "Shara." We started to talk, first about the weather, then about music and movies, then about pets—she was a dog person, while I had had a black cat as a boy. Then about our jobs. She was a psychiatrist, and I thought, *Excellent, I need one of those.* Finally, we worked our way to the wedding ring on my finger.

I explained that my wife was busy elsewhere.

"So do you have some time? I want to go dancing."

I hesitated, wondering what she had in mind.

"Just dancing, that's all," she said. "Don't you like to dance? You seem like a dancer."

I agreed, and so we hopped in a cab, and I took her to one of the clubs in town. It seemed an eternity since I had painted the town. On the ride over, I began telling her stories I had heard about Boston landmarks. Finally at the club, flashing lights; loud, thumping music; loose clothing and bodies. I was enjoying myself enough that I forgot to ask what she was doing cruising bars for male companionship.

Shara possessed an exotic flair. She made me feel alive, connected. In another time, another universe, I could have fallen for her. Her hypnotizing stare. Her disarming smile. Her smoky voice. Her raven hair, matted with sweat. Her figure, accented in all the right places by a tiny, black dress that seemed inadequate to contain her perfect breasts. Even the lines in her face, around her lips and eyes, they enhanced the character of her personality. She shot tremors through my heart, vibrating down my spine, and into my groin.

I didn't remember the last time Gail and I had made love, and I wondered—just hypothetically—how far I would be willing to go, if Shara were interested in more than just dancing. I had no intention of making a move, even if she were to hint that she was interested, and she had thrown no hints.

Taking a break, we sat at the bar and watched the other dancers and yelled at each other, the club substitution for talking. In order to hear what each other said, we leaned in closer, close enough that I could smell her hair, could have nibbled on her ear.

Shara stood and took my hand is if to drag me out to the dance floor again. I moved to stand, but before I dropped off the edge of my barstool, she turned toward me, stared into my eyes with that sultry look I will forever associate with her, wrapped my hand around her waist.

I don't remember who made the first move. If she, I bore equal guilt, because I had readily responded. Either way, I had not consciously acted, had not thought about what I was doing. I literally discovered myself kissing her, as in an erotic dream, while she rubbed her body against my crotch in time to the music. I wanted to take her to my bed, undress her, so we could enjoy each other.

I suddenly caught hold of my senses, the music still pounding around us. I pulled away, pushed her away. In my mind, everyone was staring. In reality, they probably weren't: Most of the patrons were more interested in the partners they were with. The others would avert their eyes out of politeness or embarrassment, or thought we were just dancing.

I apologized, as best I could through the din, apologized that I couldn't go on with what I had started, because I was married.

She smiled lightheartedly and said, "That's okay. I'm not looking for a relationship, just a little fun."

I explained that I couldn't do this anymore *at all*, because I loved my wife. Surprising me, she seemed to understand. Apparently, she had had some experience at picking up married men.

I rode home alone, debating whether I would tell Gail what had happened or not. On the one hand, she probably deserved to know that I had been unfaithful to her. And I wanted to come clean with her, to assuage my own conscience. On the other hand, there was no affair, no sleeping around behind her back. And our marriage was headed for the edge, and this incident would push it over. But what damage had I already done to our relationship by cheating on her? Gail deserved to know what was going on inside of me. Could I tell her that without revealing the whole truth? And thereby, would I be doing her any favors? I went back and forth between telling her and keeping it a secret, for almost an hour, the entire way home.

Then instead of going in, I stood outside our building. I decided to take a short walk to clear my head. Instead of clearing, my mind filled many times over with the same thoughts and feelings.

I finally arrived home, again, muddled and confused.

Gail was snoring rhythmically in bed. I stood for a moment, staring at her beautiful forever-young face, poking out from under the covers. And I felt sorry for myself for missing her, and sorry for her that I had missed her. Without waking her, I showered and changed, and I snuggled up next to her, wrapping my leg around hers, caressing her arm with my hand. She felt warm and soft, like a kitten, and I loved her dearly.

I decided I could not hurt her any more than I already had. I would keep the events of that evening a secret forever. And I would make it up to her the next morning.

———

After Gail stormed out of the cottage, she walked a ways up Ardor Road, away from the point. To her left, she could see the colors of the sunset over the bay through the trees. At any other time, the beauty of the scene would have overwhelmed her, but at the moment she simply wasn't in the mood for beautiful. On her right, she approached one of the numerous houses on the peninsula.

I wonder how much these places cost? she wondered. *How did George's folks even afford a cottage here?*

What had gotten into George? What had gotten into Ann? "Every relationship I have in this place is crazy," she said out loud to herself. "George starts talking romantic and drives me half out of my senses. Then Ann starts trash-talking. I see now why I moved away!"

All she wanted was a little respect. She wasn't one of

George's "bodies," and she wasn't just an appendage to the people around her. Her life had meaning, and they needed to acknowledge that.

She glanced up and noticed a middle-aged gentleman staring at her curiously from his work in the garage of the house she had been passing.

"Hello," she said, as though nothing were strange.

"Hello," he replied, cautiously.

And she marched on.

———

After Gail stormed out of the cottage, Eddie confronted his mother. He insisted on knowing what the argument was about. What had set Ann and Gail against each other? Did it have anything to do with what they were talking about before he had returned?

The only answer he got was, "I expect that relationship won't last long."

After another hour, Gail entered the cottage, ignored his hello, and went straight to her room.

That night, he couldn't sleep. He sat on the couch, a war documentary on the television, silently sipping clear liquid from a whiskey glass. On the end table next to him stood a half-empty bottle of vodka, which he stared at instead of watching the TV, occasionally tracing the outline of the label with his finger.

Out of nowhere, Bob plopped into the chair across from him and slammed down his own glass on the table.

Eddie started. "Sorry, I didn't hear you come in. Want some?"

"Astounding. Like you could read my mind!"

Eddie silently poured him a shot.

"How come you get all the fun, huh?" Bob grabbed the bottle and filled his cup as full as Eddie's. He held up his cup. "To our women!" and swigged.

"Cheers," Eddie mumbled without moving.

"What are we watching?"

"A World War II documentary. Hitler has just invaded the Soviet Union." Eddie watched war documentaries to distract his thoughts. This was the horror that was the human condition, man against man, people against people, ready to fight to the death for ideology or land or even for a piece of cloth flapping in the smoke-drenched wind.

"Looks like you're going to run out of vodka before the war is over," Bob said in a mock Russian accent.

"Don't worry. Got another bottle in the cabinet." Eddie took a swig.

"Okay," Bob said. "Level. What's going on?"

"I'm watching TV is what's going on." And trying to distract himself from Gail, he thought, just long enough to fall asleep.

"Is this about Ann and Gail?"

"Yeah, that too," he said. He hated it when his loved ones fought. Much better to watch the world leaders duke it out with other peoples' blood, than to watch your own friends crap all over their friendships and not be able to do anything to stop it.

"You know, these guys," Eddie said, motioning to the television— He only had a vague idea of what he wanted to say. He started again. "When did wars become about who was right and who was wrong? It's bad enough to have to go to war to defend yourself. But somewhere 'defense' turned into an ideology. I think there are things that are more important than ideology."

"Maybe," Bob said, nodding.

Bob remained neutral on most political issues, while Eddie was a peacenik. Where did Bob stand, if he stood anywhere? Bob contented himself with letting others work out their own political issues. Eddie could understand that. He too hated to argue politics. But Bob never seemed to get upset, even if the world was falling apart around him, even if his own wife was in the middle of a knock-out-drag-down fight with her business partner. Bob had perfected a peace of mind that kept his sanity while all around Eddie was losing his.

"Sometimes, my old friend, I wish I could be as nonchalant about war as you are."

"Old friends are the best kind," Bob said.

"To old friends!" Eddie rose his glass.

"Hear hear," said Bob, raising his own, and they both drank.

"I think I'm in love with her, you know," Eddie said.

"Yeah," Bob said, "I thought there might have been something happening there when you invited her up for the weekend."

"Actually, that was just a friendly gesture. But out on the beach this afternoon..." Eddie sighed. A half-truth, but true enough for Eddie's conscience.

"So what's the problem? I know you're not shy. You've certainly been with enough women."

Too true, Eddie thought. But Gail was not just another woman. She was special. And she was his ex-wife, with enough history to mix him up but good. And she wasn't sharing her feelings with him; that didn't help clarify anything. But one thing he did know: he would be devastated if she rejected him.

"You don't get it," Eddie said. "I'm *in love* with her. She's not just a woman. She's..." Eddie couldn't find the words. "I haven't felt this way in a long, long time."

His years with Gail excited him, at least in the beginning. They had been growing together. Their relationship wasn't sexual, even though her beauty still amazed him. They had more than romance. They simply were. He and Gail never really saw eye to eye, but he loved her just the same, always and forever. For all of her yin to his yang, he both loathed and admired her. He always and only wanted to make her happy. And he would always regret having let her go.

He went back to watching the documentary.

"What are you going to do?" Bob asked.

"Don't know," Eddie said, eyes still on the television.

"You do know that no matter what happens, you can't find what you're looking for in there," pointing to the bottle.

"But," Eddie said, "maybe it'll help me feel a little better, just for a little while. Help me think."

"Is it helping?"

No it wasn't, but Eddie didn't admit it. Instead, he took another drink. Maybe if he kept trying, something would break for him. He simply didn't feel like trying anything else right now.

"You're going to talk to her about it, right?" Bob said.

Eddie shifted his gaze to his friend and saw there an almost-panicked looked on his face. The only man in the world who was more easy-going than Eddie was panicked about Gail?

"Why?" Eddie asked.

"Because," Bob said. He returned to watching the TV himself. "I just think you should go for it." He took another swig. "Otherwise, how can you expect to get what you want?"

"Yeah, I know that," Eddie said. "But it's not that simple. Gail is... different."

"I got that impression. Look"—he turned to stare Eddie straight in the eye—"you want a commitment with her, right?"

Eddie thought about that word *commitment*. Is that what he wanted? He had been married once. Didn't really try to find commitment back then; it just sort of found him. He didn't know what he wanted. He just wanted Gail.

"You want something like what you had before."

Again, that wasn't quite right. What they had before wasn't that great. Eddie wanted something different than what they had before, better than what they had before.

When Eddie didn't answer, Bob tried a different tack. "You love her, right?"

"Yes." That much was obvious.

"Why is it so important for you to love Gail?"

"Because she was my life. I owe her." Eddie hadn't realized that maybe he felt a little guilty for letting her slip away the first time. Maybe he actually was trying to get back what he had before.

"What do you owe her for?" Bob asked.

Eddie just shook his head. He didn't want to rehash the past. He just wanted a brighter future, and he couldn't see one coming.

"Well, you can hardly start off on the right foot by hiding your true feelings from her. How do you expect to get what you want, if you're dishonest with her about it?"

"But if I tell her how I feel, I may lose her," he admitted. "I may never see her again."

"Then maybe you'll never see her again. But you can't go on lying to her like this. If you're that deeply in love with her, she has to be told."

Eddie shook his head. "I couldn't stand to lose her again."

"Do you even have her now?"

Chapter Thirteen

*E*ddie awoke early, energized, and without a hangover. Endorphins pumping through his system, he felt as though he had experienced a spiritual reawakening. *This must be,* he thought, *how holy rollers feel after a charismatic revival service.*

In Eddie's case, he hadn't rediscovered God so much as having rediscovered the will to love. In a moment of clarity, he had realized that he hadn't been seeking love, true love—except with Gail. He had been looking for romance, a little sex, fun times and fast women, no attachments, no regrets. But Gail represented attachment. She would never be just another woman to him. And if he let her pass through his fingers again, she would become a double regret. He couldn't let that happen.

He would level with Gail about how he felt and what he wanted. So often while they were married, he hadn't, and that's why their relationship had declined and fallen. If he hoped to win her back, he must come clean with her, no matter how it unnerved him, because by doing so, he could turn things around.

Eddie heard her creaking down the old stairs after he

had been up for hours, shopping, baking, and now making her breakfast.

As Gail descended the narrow staircase, the sound of swing music and scent of fried clams grew stronger, infusing her with comfort and warmth. She hadn't eaten fried clams for breakfast since she had been married. At first, they had cold clam roll Sunday morning, left over from the romantic night before. George used to joke about clams being "the other aphrodisiac shellfish." The ritual progressed to fresh, homemade fried clams instead of eggs and bacon, accompanied by swing music, because that just happened to be what was in the CD player. Even after the relationship started to fizzle out, at least they still had fried clams and swing music.

She padded into the kitchen, grinning at George, who was slaving over a sizzling frying pan.

"Good morning, sleepyhead," he said.

"G'd m'rning," she mumbled. "Aren't you supposed to be the one who sleeps in?" She had always awoken at the break of dawn, while he had always overslept. And here she was, the morning half gone already. It had been a long time since she had slept in, and the experience refreshed and relaxed her. She assumed that everyone one else was out, maybe walking along the beach, maybe boating, or maybe even at church.

The strong, succulent aroma of clams blended with a different, fluffier, yeastier smell, like that of a bakery. She turned to see a loaf of piping hot bread cooling on a rack on the counter.

"Fresh bread!" she shouted, jarring Eddie nearly out of his sandals.

"Careful," he warned playfully. "Man with hot skillet here."

She sidled up to him and said, "Where did you get fresh baked bread from?"

"I made that."

"Since when?" she said. George had never been much the cook. There were a few dishes he had learned to make, like the clams, but he would never have braved something like bread, that required measuring and mixing and kneading and rising and baking.

"Hey, I know how to do stuff."

"Like bake bread?"

"Like use a bread machine," he said.

"Smells delicious." She was quickly realizing how empty her stomach was. She had not had a proper dinner the prior evening, and now she'd almost missed breakfast.

Eddie recognized the cooing in her voice, recognized it as delight. "Good. I'm glad you like it."

He dumped the last batch of clams onto the rack to cool and turned to face her. She was wearing a frumpy, flannel nightshirt under a powder blue robe with matching slippers. She was not wearing any makeup, and her hair was mussed, matted on one side and sticking out on the other. He reached out his hand and patted down the hair where it stood on end, and gazed affectionately at her.

"You're still pretty, first thing in the morning," he said.

"Thank you," she said, flattered and appreciative. "I'm starved!" Her eyes grew wide with excitement.

———

George and I made love for the last time on a Sunday morning. I had been studying late the previous night, and George hadn't come home, not until very late. I finally went to bed at one or two in the morning.

The next thing I knew, I awoke to the smell of fried clams and the sound of swing music. George had revived our Sunday morning breakfast tradition, it would turn out, for one last Sunday morning.

I had overslept. It must have been 10:00. Not that I had anything scheduled for Sunday morning, but I had a big test coming up, which is why I had been studying so hard the night before. I expected it to be a busy weekend.

Somewhere between bed and breakfast, however, I relaxed. George spoke to me affectionately, convinced me that I'd do better on the test if I took a break and spent some time goofing off. His craziness sometimes allowed me to loosen up and be crazy, too.

He served us fresh clam rolls. We ate. Then we danced in the living room. We laughed. George pressed his body against mine. His arms wrapping around me, he held me, and it had been too long since he last held me like that. He caressed my cheek with his hand and leaned in and kissed me.

Before I knew it, he was exploring my body on the living room floor, and I his. His body covered mine like a blanket, his kisses sprinkled their way down my neck and over my lips.

We felt so... together, in the moment together. That's the only way I can think of to describe it.

———

Eddie sawed off two thick slices of soft, steaming bread, careful not to crush it in the process, placed one on each of two plates, and heaped the breaded clams on top. He also poured two glasses of sparkling lemon water.

Seeing George serve her breakfast like this struck Gail with mixed feelings. The setting reminded her of him, of the good times. For a moment, she wondered if they could get away with sex on his parents' couch, or if someone would walk in on them. Then she caught herself. She was not a piece of meat, and there was no relationship. She needed to keep a proper arm's length.

But she still wanted to thank him.

He staggered toward the dining room, two plates of food precariously balanced in one hand, the other holding the glasses of water, but she was in his way. And she neither turned nor move.

"Uh, I thought we'd eat in there." He looked toward the

dining area.

She stood on her tippy-toes and kissed him on the cheek. "Thank you," she said. Then she sat at the table, leaving him toothy like a clown statue.

Eddie was now more sure of his mission, now more than ever.

He met her at the table. "I miss times like this."

"Me too," Gail replied. Full of enjoyment.

"I miss you." Sober.

Gail gazed up at him. She had to admit, that he had added something to her life, for as long as he was in it. A little dazed, "Me, too," she said.

"I've been wondering whether we could make it, if we tried again, now that everything's different." That was the toned-down version, toned down as far as he could. Inside, all he could think of how much he desperately wanted her to say "Me, too" again.

Gail had briefly played with the idea, but her thoughts were still ill-formed. All she knew clearly was that she neither wanted to hurt him again nor to get hurt. She didn't want a repeat of what happened before, and she was convinced that's what she would get if she allowed anything between them.

She found herself shaking her head. "I don't think so," she said, level-voiced, professional. "We'd just end up where we were before. I like it better this way, as friends." Just saying it made her feel better. It was indeed better this way, better than when they were married. Now they could lead their separate lives, grow close, but not be at odds with each other.

Eddie's heart was reeling. "We're different people now, not like it was before. Don't you think that it could be different now? After all these years? Why do you think it would be the same?"

She didn't really know how she knew it would be the same, but she did. "I just do." She didn't want to hurt him, but she didn't see she had any choice. Sleeping with him would just complicate everything.

The situation was beginning to frustrate Eddie. This wasn't how it was supposed to go. "You're not giving me much to go on, here," he said, keeping his voice as steady as he possibly could.

"I'm sorry." She didn't want to argue with him, but she just couldn't go there. She didn't want to lose what they had.

Eddie took a deep breath. Relax. Regroup. "It's okay," he said. "It's just a thought that had crossed my mind. I like having you as a friend, too." He touched her hand from across the table, smiled coolly into her eyes. Maybe her mind would change. There was always hope. There always had to be hope, Eddie thought, because hope sustained him. It was all he had left.

They finished breakfast, talking about light subjects. The weather report—they expected it to be sunny. The beach. The Porters, whom Gail liked very much. Plans for the afternoon. Swimming, if Gail wanted. Eddie offered to take Gail out on his father's Laser.

"On his what?"

"Laser," Eddie repeated. "Sailboat. That's probably where he and Bob are now. I think Mom and Ann went shopping in town."

On the stereo, the song "Manhattan" by Steve Tyrell started playing. Gail jumped up. "Ooh! I love this song!" It post-dated their marriage, but she had heard it somewhere. "Let's dance," she said.

George knew how to dance. He took her hand and led her around the floor, out the back door, and onto the enclosed porch, where there was more room. They were both enjoying themselves. Gail rarely got to dance anymore, even at weddings, which she rarely was invited to. And Eddie missed dancing with Gail.

As the song ended, he pulled her close to him.

He kissed her.

This time, she did not kiss back. She caught herself in time and pushed away.

Her dismay turned to fury. They had agreed, no funny stuff. They had agreed to be friends. Friends *without* so-called benefits. She thought they were on the same page. Now, he had crossed the line. That was unacceptable.

He saw the rage etched into her face. "I'm sorry," he gushed. "I lost my senses for a moment. Please, don't be mad."

"Look. If you can't handle us being just friends...
Maybe we just shouldn't hang out together any more,
Eddie."

That was the first time she had called him "Eddie."
She spoke the name with an edge sharp enough to cut
glass.

And she stormed out.

Chapter Fourteen

*E*ddie stood, in shock, for a moment. His brain stopped thinking. The next song was playing on the stereo, another happy, romantic song appropriate for dancing. But Eddie, all alone now, felt not much like dancing. He didn't feel like anything. His system had shut down. Catatonia.

He needed to shut off the music, because the music made him feel, and he needed not to feel. He managed to find the remote control for the stereo, which he had left on the couch end table. Silenced the cacophony.

Still in a daze, he fell into a porch chair, stared out at the trees behind the house, watched their branches sway ever so slightly, slowly, as if in a dream. He sat there for a long time, just dwelling in the gentle rustling of the leaves, the cool lapping of the breeze against his skin.

Finally, grief fell upon him. And grief gave way to helplessness; and helplessness, to torment; and torment, to tears; and tears, to sobs; and sobs, to exhaustion. He breathed deeply, laboriously, closed his swollen eyes, drifted toward sleep. He found enough strength to shuffle into the living room and lie on the couch.

———

Gail marched down East Ardor Road, toward the beach. She didn't know where she was going. She was simply going, fuming again, and she wouldn't stop until she calmed down.

She should never have come. She had been demeaned, degraded, and ignored. Eddie should have known better. *Eddie,* Gail thought, *the name suits him.* Fun-loving is one thing, but she needed a friend, and in return, he made a pass at her. She might have understood if he hadn't known, but she told him exactly what she wanted, and he agreed. He should have respected that. Instead, he crossed the line, invaded her space, invaded her life.

And the worst part, she felt betrayed. Like most women, she had dealt with enough idiot men throughout the years. But George was supposed to be different. He was supposed to be her friend.

Damn!

"Hey, Missy," called a familiar voice, though Gail at first couldn't identify it.

Gail swung her head toward the sound. The dear, old Mr. Porter had pulled his grill out onto his driveway and was wearing a large apron with stylized lettering: "Over 60 and still cookin'!" The wind shifted, sending a whiff of hot charcoal through her nostrils.

"Where're you, goin' in such a hurry?" he said. "Anything I can, help with?"

Gail took a deep breath and sighed. "No," she said. "I

was just out for a walk."

He stepped closer to her and lowered his voice. "I think, the whole neighborhood heard, that you and, 'Eddie' aren't, 'hanging out together,' anymore." His voice returned to normal volume. "I don't understand, you young people. 'Hanging out'? What does, that mean? Is that—"

"That means," Gail said, interrupting, "that George and I probably aren't friends anymore." Were they ever really friends? Or was his friendship just a pretext to get her into a compromising position? "Or *will* never be good friends." Even that didn't feel right. "Or something."

She wasn't sure what she and George were or would ever be. They were exes, and maybe that was it. You're not actually supposed to stay friends with your ex, are you? Yes, you *say* you're going to remain friends. But a new love always comes along, and you move on, and you lose touch, and then you decide you don't actually want to talk to him anymore. Because you can't just be friends, can you? You'll always be either lovers or nothing. Thank God there were no kids involved, because their divorce was clean, uncluttered, without attachments, no complications. She and George met again after all these years by chance, a stupid coincidence. It was never supposed to happen that way, and the whole thing just got screwed up.

Lola arrived with a plate of raw hamburger patties

and a bag of hamburger rolls. "Oh, are we having a guest? I should make some more."

"No," Gail said. "I was just passing by."

"That's fine," she said, smiling. "Honey, since you're here, can you help me with something inside? It'll only take a minute."

What could she possibly need Gail's help with? This woman might have been old, but she had vigor, strength, capability, probably more so than Gail.

"I can give you a hand," Mr. Porter said.

"No, Frank. You need to watch your charcoals smolder, or whatever you do out here." Turning to Gail, "It's a man thing."

Mr. Porter chuckled.

Lola ushered Gail into their living room and offered her a seat on the couch.

"I don't understand," Gail said. "I thought—"

"Just sit."

Gail did, and Lola sat beside her.

"I'm sorry to say," Lola said, "that your voice carries."

"I'm so sorry," said Gail. She felt her face turn red. "I didn't mean to— But I was—"

"You were upset, and you didn't think that the neighbors would be listening."

"It won't happen again," she said. That was the truth. She would never return here again. That would at least make living down the situation easier.

"Do you want to talk about it?"

Gail shook her head. Though she did want to talk, she had expected to make up with Ann. But in the moment, she wished she had a sympathetic ear. "I don't know."

"George obviously cares about you, and I'm willing to help in any way that I can."

If George had cared about her, he would have respected her boundaries. Gail scrunched up her face. "George only cares about one thing. You said it yourself."

The elder woman looked confused. "What happened?"

"He made a pass at me."

"And you didn't want him to?"

Why would she have wanted him to? "Of course not."

Lola nodded. "And he knew you didn't want him to."

Lola understood, or at least she was asking all the right questions. That's what Gail needed right now.

"We discussed it," Gail said. "We agreed: just friends. No funny stuff. And then he goes and does this."

"I see," said Lola. "I'm sorry to hear that you don't feel the same way about him. Because he needs someone like you in his life."

This conversation felt familiar. She had said that once before. But what was the point? Gail couldn't change the way she felt, nor the truth of the situation. Having a relationship with him under these circumstances was unfathomable. "Are you saying that I should let him, uh..."

"No, Sweetie." She gave Gail a warm, caring smile. "I was just pontificating. It's a bad habit of mine."

Gail could see that she was genuinely concerned. "That's not pontificating. You just care about George as much as I do."

The old woman nodded her head. "Well, Gail, I just wanted you to know that if you ever want to talk, I'm here to listen."

"George actually did have someone like me in his life once."

"You mean his ex-wife? Did you know her?"

Gail floundered in the irony. She nodded, staring at the carpet, a golden yellow that fit in with the flax and brown scheme of the walls and furniture. "Uh. Yes," Gail said. "I knew her."

"What was she like?"

"She was..." Gail stared straight into Lola's blue eyes. "Exactly like me."

Lola pondered that for a moment. Then realization eased over her face. "You mean..."

Gail nodded. "I was... the ex-wife."

Gail could see the neurons firing in Lola's brain. Gail was a little surprised that she had never even suspected a previous relationship. But she guessed that the pattern must have been too clear, too regular, since then. He never kept a relationship with any girl he wasn't sleeping with, and if he wasn't sleeping with Gail, then all rules were off.

"And now," Lola said, "George wants to revive the relationship, but you don't."

Gail comprehended the tension in that statement. "It just couldn't work," Gail said. "It ended badly before, and it would just end badly again."

"What happened? ...if you don't mind talking about it. George never talks about it. He talks about all the other girls, even right to their face, talks about other girls he's slept with, which I always thought was in poor taste. But he never mentions you. And every time we've asked him, he changes the subject."

He'd never mentioned any other woman to her or around her. Maybe she really was different than other women. So then why couldn't he keep it in his pants?

"He never talks about me," Gail said.

"No. Everything we know about George's marriage, we've heard from his parents. That's how I know she was — you were a good influence on him."

Dad Chase had glowed when he first saw her at the cottage. "They've always been great to me. Generous and kind."

"They're good people, and we're lucky to have them as neighbors."

"But Mom— that is, Mrs. Chase seems to be uncomfortable with me being there."

Lola pursed her lips. "Have you ever talked to her

about the divorce?"

Before this weekend, she had not talked to them at all. In any case, she had assumed it to be an uncomfortable subject. Only over the past day had she even considered broaching the subject. "No, we've never discussed it. I haven't even seen them since before George and I broke up."

"They say when parents divorce, it's hard on the kids. But what they don't usually mention is that when kids divorce, it can be just as hard on the parents."

Gail had never considered that before, that George's mother had not dealt with the separation. "My parents were very supportive of me, as long as I was happy and doing well. They used to call me, badger me about it. Sometimes, they were downright annoying."

"Maybe they needed to feel that you were alright, for their own peace of mind."

Gail agreed. "Some part of me always knew that this was how they were dealing with what I was going through. In a way, they needed moral support from me. And I guess they got it. But maybe..." Maybe, Gail thought, Mom Chase never got that from George.

"Or maybe," Lola said, "your folks would make George feel the same way you do now, not intentionally, just because it would be a strange situation."

Gail wondered how her parents would react to George being a part of her life again, after all these years. She

honestly didn't know. Until recently, she had not
considered it, and she had not talked to them about the
idea.

"When a child divorces," Lola continued, "there's a
grieving process the parent goes through. And it can be
very lonely, too, because everyone expects them to just
deal with it. In a way, it's like a member of the family has
died. And now, it must be like you've come back to life
again, but not you, not the same you, because you two
aren't married anymore. It's bound to be uncomfortable."

"So I should talk to them about this," Gail said.

"Well, I don't see the point in digging up old wounds.
But if you're going to be a part of their lives, a part of
George's life, you might at least want to get that out in
the open, talk to them about your relationship and what it
means. Otherwise, it's bound to cause stress. Of course,
first you have to figure out what relationship you have
with George."

Chapter Fifteen

I was in middle school, 11 years old, and he was going into high school. That first crush, I handled it so badly. But Michael was tall, taller than any other boy in class, and cute, and he sat beside me in English class. He had smooth hands and medium-length, light brown hair that ended in little, curled wisps. I longed to hear his voice, and the teacher frequently called on him to read some poem or paragraph of prose, because he had a strong, solid voice, but smooth as satin. Once, he read a poem about a blind man who sees the woman he's in love with by touching her with his hands. And I imagined that he was reading not to the class but to me personally, and I fantasized about what it would be like to have his hands touch me.

But he didn't even know I existed. Or so I thought, until I happened to meet up with him after school. We walked down across the schoolyard and toward the baseball field. Actually, he walked, and I followed. But I would have followed him to Siberia and back. I don't remember all of what we talked about, but I do remember the sound of his voice. And I remember how he made me feel, excited and uneasy and happy all at the same time.

We reached the edge of the field, and he sat down on the grass and began to fiddle with a dandelion. We ended up laying there on our stomachs, in the hot, green grass, playing with the wild flora, sharing our thoughts with one another.

I was telling him about my homework, when right in the middle of a sentence, he hopped to his feet and started away. I couldn't see where he was going, until I sat up and noticed that he had walked over to meet a girl, a blonde with straight, long hair and smooth, fair skin. I had seen her around school before, but I didn't know her name. She had filled out more than I had, and she was wearing a delicate, powder blue sweater and designer jeans, all of which showed off her ample figure. How could I compete with that?

He kissed her on the lips, right out there in public. And I could almost hear my heart rip inside my chest.

I remember him waving goodbye to me just before they strolled away, hand in hand. I also remember her withering glare, which turned into jealousy and anger inside me.

After that, we still talked from time to time in class. Once, he even asked me what was bothering me. What was bothering me was the way I felt about him. I never forgave him for breaking my heart. I see now that he had done nothing wrong. He had not misled me. He had not led me on. He had not asked me out. I had simply been infatuated, and my infatuation had gotten away from me.

Years later, I met him again in high school. He and the other girl had broken up. For all I know, he may have had dozens of girlfriends in that time. But I no longer cared. I needed not to care. We still spoke, politely, and he even asked me to go with him. But I told him, "No, because I just don't feel that way about you."

In reality, part of me was still hurting.

———

"I don't know, Lola," Gail said. "What are George and I?"

"I thought you said you were friends."

"I did say that. But..."

Gail told her about their trip to the beach the previous day, about her romantic feelings, about her apology to him for her part in letting their marriage slip away, about his apology to her, about starting over, about how sad and confused she felt. "Is that even possible, to start over? As if nothing ever happened?"

"Oh, yes. People do it all the time. Usually with different partners. But they repeat the same mistakes, the same story over and over again. But it sounds to me he doesn't really want to start over. He wants to try something different."

"But why should I feel sad? After all these years?"

"Maybe he's not just a friend to you? Maybe he's something more?"

Gail shook her head. "It wouldn't matter. We're too

different. We'd just end up fighting and breaking up again. And I don't think I could handle that again."

"Well, that may well be, but I don't really know anything about it. I think a lot of couples break up simply because they drift apart. It's not because of the fighting that they divorce. The fighting is just a symptom, like the sniffles is a symptom of a cold. You can treat the runny nose, but your body still needs to get over the virus before you'll be well again. But they never get over their virus. Because they've stopped finding satisfaction in each other, they look elsewhere."

She was pontificating again. "The couples who stay together, like Frank and I, we've learned how to forgive, and to talk to each other."

"That's similar to what happened to George and me," Gail said. "We just became less and less important to each other. We started living our own lives, because we had our own interests. And I don't see that being any different now. I have my business that I'm trying to go forward with. He has his family and friends." Gail remembered one more thing. "And his women." Envy rippled through her body. Why should she be envious?

"I don't know what he's doing with that," Lola said. "What's he looking for? I imagine he's broken more than a few hearts. Maybe he's looking for magic. You want some advice?"

"Sure," Gail said, out of respect. She didn't have to

listen to the advice if she didn't want to.

"There's no magic," Lola said. "Fairy tales are just that, fairy tales. If you want to be happy in a relationship, you have to accept each other the way they are, and you have to build new experiences on the good things you have together, and sometimes you even have to just stick with it until it gets good."

"Exactly," Gail said. "That's why our relationship failed, because we didn't have that, and I don't want to do that again."

"So you're saying you don't want to get married, as George seems to want."

Gail did not think that George wanted to get married again. "What makes you think he wants me to marry him?"

"Well, what else would he want? From that story you told me, it sounded like he wanted a relationship like what you had before, except one that works."

"I don't know how I feel about that," Gail said.

"Well, you probably feel scared and confused, and maybe even overwhelmed."

This woman could see into Gail's soul, creepy, as though she were a bona fide psychic, or as if she had done it all before and was speaking from experience.

"Do you feel comfortable starting this business with Ann?" Lola switched gears, but Gail had a psychology degree and could see the metaphor she was getting at.

"Yes." For the most part, that was true, except that she and Ann sometimes didn't see eye to eye, and that concerned her. "And excited. There's always something exciting about starting a new project. I see where you're going, but—"

"What about your first business? Same thing?"

It surely did excite her, but it wasn't as comfortable. Back then, she only partially knew what she was doing. She didn't know whether she would succeed or whether she would fall flat on her face, end up crawling back to Mommy and Daddy with her hand out.

"Yes," Gail said. "Same thing, except I didn't know what was going to happen, because I had never done it before. But marrying George, I've done that before."

"That's the business you started after the company you were with before went bankrupt?"

Were her expectations of a future with George colored by her past relationship with him? Yes, of course they were! "I see what you're getting at, but George and I are sure to run into the same problems that we had before. After all, for all that's different, it's still essentially the same situation."

"I'm not talking about George anymore." Mrs. Potter's eyes took on a wise, knowing look, as if they had seen something in Gail's mind that Gail was too close to discern. She took a breath and began. "It sounds like you established a pattern, that relationships took second importance to your career. Is that right?"

"Yes, but that's just where I was at."

"Have you had any long-term relationships since then?"

"No. That's just not where my priorities were. There's nothing wrong with that," Gail objected.

"I agree," the old woman said. "There's nothing wrong with that if it makes you happy, if that's the life you want to live. When I was your age, society told women what to expect of their lives. We were to get married and raise a family, and so forth. Today, you girls have so many more options available to you. And that's wonderful.

"But it also means you have to choose. If you put everything into your career, that means you'll never have a long-term relationship, and you'll never be married, at least not successfully. And if that's what you want, that's what you should choose. It sounds like that's what you have chosen. The only question is whether or not you want a change."

That struck Gail in the gut. It clarified everything. That couldn't be right, could it? Not with regard to George. What about all of the circumstances? All the baggage between them? All the reasons why it could never work?

"But even if I do want a change," Gail said, "that doesn't mean George is the right man for me."

"Sweetie, there is no 'right' man. You find someone

who's willing to make an honest go at it with you, and then you take the plunge. And it's just like when you started your first business. And when it works out, then it becomes something special."

Gail didn't know whether she could accept that it was really that easy. No, not easy: simple. But she had done this already in her career. She remembered the decision to strike out on her own. It wasn't easy, and she knew it wouldn't be. But the decision was simple, because it was the obvious choice.

She would have to think about this further.

Chapter Sixteen

*E*ddie awoke slowly to voices.

"He didn't sleep well last night." Bob's voice.

"Looks like he and Gail had lunch, though." Dad.

"And I see you were nice enough to clean up." Mom.

The rustle of plastic shopping bags.

"Bob does the same thing at home." Ann. "Leaves dirty dishes all over the place. I once found a used cereal bowl underneath the bed!"

"Yes, I'm a slob."

Eddie shifted, but he kept his eyes closed. The welling of tears had long since passed, but he still didn't want to face anyone. Didn't want to explain. He also didn't know where Gail was or how much time had passed, but he thought maybe he might be able to gain a clue or two by listening in.

"And it smelled," Ann continued. "I changed those sheets three times before I figured out where the smell was coming from. I thought there was something wrong with my laundry. But, no! It was you!"

A pause.

"Well, maybe," Mom said, "if you two can put your affections on hold, then Ann and I can start dinner. And you boys can clean up in here."

"Yes, my dear," Dad said, and Eddie could see the old man's teeth even through his eyelids.

"Should we wake George?" Mom said.

"No, let him sleep."

He drifted back into his dreams, until he heard Bob and Ann arguing, whispering hoarsely, harshly.

"You told me not to meddle," Ann scolded, "and then you stick your big nose into it."

"I wasn't meddling," Bob shot back, clearly annoyed by the reference to the size of his nose. Ann loved him, and even loved his nose, but Bob was still sensitive about it. "I saw a friend in pain, and I talked to him, that's all. And what about all the pressure you put on Gail? You weren't meddling? You think that didn't backfire?"

"And you set him up to go down, too," Ann continued as though Bob hadn't said anything. "What kind of friend is that?"

"That's nonsense."

"You pushed him into making a move without knowing how she would respond. You should have asked me about it first."

"Look, he had to go for it, resolve it one way or the other. It's what I would do. It's what he would do."

"You just don't get it, do you?"

As each shot was fired, Eddie felt more dragged down. He should have just stayed in bed that morning, rather than to have caused so much trouble. That way, at least he'd be the only one suffering. Now, at least three of his friends were suffering, and maybe upset with him as well.

Eddie shifted on the couch. The voices instantaneously stopped. Two pairs of shoes clopped away.

———

Gail spent the afternoon with the Porters. She politely turned down lunch, explaining that she had a big, late breakfast, but she nibbled on a salad so that she could sit and chat with them during lunch. She just needed a break from the drama. Afterward, she walked down toward the point, stopping at a park bench overlooking the dock. She sat there for some time, thinking about nothing in partic- ular, and watching a dinghy floating in the water, the current causing it to bump it over and over again into the dock, in a sort of hypnotic rhythm, slowly, soothing. *Bump. Ba-dump. Bump. Bump. Ba-dump.* Like the thumping of her heart against the world.

Afterward, on the way to the point, she passed a middle-aged gentleman, well dressed, but casually, in a polo shirt and trousers, strolling the opposite way carrying an umbrella, even though above them stretched a cloudless sky. Give him a suit coat and top hat, Gail thought, and he'd look like something out of 19'th century London. He greeted her politely, grinning broadly, and she returned the greeting.

When she reached the beach, she sat on a rock overlooking it while the summer sun arced away from its peak overhead toward the western horizon. Gail imagined the evening twilight sun against the trees in the distance. She might be able to stay and see it, just before she had to leave, probably never to return. The thought imbued her with a sense of loss, but whatever she had lost, maybe she had lost it long ago.

A woman and two young girls visited the beach, escorting a short-haired terrier, brown and white, with cute little ears that flapped as he hopped along. The girls took off their sandals, waded in the tidal pools, and talked about the seaweed lapping against the sand. Meanwhile, the dog hopped up to Gail, wagging its tail and yipping excitedly.

"Here, Rusty!" the woman called. She wore her hair short and straight and dark, and the strains of motherhood were beginning to etch lines onto her face, under her eyes and around her mouth.

"I'm sorry," she said to Gail. "I hope he didn't disturb you. He's harmless, just playful."

Gail understood and happily told her that the dog wasn't bothering her either way. Gail asked her about the man she had passed on the street, with the umbrella.

"That sounds like Mr. Keller," she said. "He owns one of the cottages down the street." She pointed further down in the direction Gail had been walking. "Are you visiting for the week?"

"Just for the weekend. We'll be going back today." Gail introduced herself, explained that she was visiting with the Chases.

"Oh, you must be a 'friend' of Eddie's." Despite her coolness, Gail heard her put quotes around the word *friend*.

"No, not of Eddie's," Gail said with a knowing leer. "Not a 'friend' of Eddie's. Actually, my girlfriend is a friend of the family."

Gail introduced herself, and the woman, herself, as "Melinda."

Melinda continued talking about Mr. Keller. "Yeah, Jeff Keller always walks with an umbrella. I don't know why. I think he's interested in Katrina Houston, whether they'll finally get together or not. You should see them flirt."

Gail giggled. "I heard about that. Why don't they just get together and be done with it?"

"Well, it's more complicated than that. They're both corporate execs, and both in competing technology companies. I guess it would look bad if they were sleeping together, sleeping with the enemy, literally.

"Add to that the fact that her last two marriages failed because she couldn't juggle work and home. I tell you, it's something else. A man works 80 hours a week, and everybody looks the other way. But a woman does the same thing, and everybody takes his side."

Gail wondered if that was true. If her and George's roles had been reversed, would their marriage have turned out differently? She doubted it, because she detected no sexism from him.

On the other hand, she was the first to mention splitting up. He wouldn't have done so. Ironically, if their roles had been reversed, maybe it *would* have turned out differently.

Gail chatted with Melinda until she noticed the light overhead begin to dim. She looked into the falling sun. Streams of red and orange rippled through clouds that she had not previously noticed.

"The sunsets here can be spectacular over the water," Melinda said.

The end of the day represented the end of an era. Not as something to dread; rather, something to look forward to, because after each restful night came a fresh, new day. She needed a fresh, new day.

———

Gail had just enough time to throw her belongings into a suitcase, grab a burger on the way out, and leap into the car, before Bob peeled out of the driveway. She barely had a chance to say goodbye to Dad Chase, much less to talk over weightier matters with him and his wife. She didn't even see George, who seemed to have disappeared. Something inside of her kept her from even asking where he was, much less leaving a message for him.

Once on the road, Gail apologized to Bob and Ann for ruining their weekend. Bob seemed perplexed.

"Isn't that why you're upset?" Gail asked him.

"No, I'm not upset." He didn't sound upset, either.

"Bob doesn't get upset," Ann explained. "Only I know how to push his buttons. And he *hates* it." Her voice had that playful lilt in it that made Gail think that they were about to start cuddling and necking and making Gail feel like a third wheel.

"Well, I'm sorry for our fight, then," she said to Ann, "for what I said to you. I've been working through some issues lately, and you got caught in the middle."

Ann returned the apology, and Gail was grateful.

"Anything you wanted to talk about?" Ann asked.

Gail wouldn't have minded sharing with Ann, but not with Bob within earshot. Even if she had known Bob better, she probably wouldn't be comfortable talking in front of him. For all she knew, anything she said might even make it back to George. She suppressed a shudder at the thought.

"Maybe a little later," Gail said.

Ann understood. "Maybe when we take a bathroom break."

"Let it go," Bob said. "If she doesn't want to talk, she doesn't want to talk."

Eventually they stopped at a rest stop along the highway. And in the relative privacy of the ladies room—

privacy from prying husbands—and waiting in line at
Starbuck's, Gail relayed to a stunned Ann what had tran-
spired that morning.

"What are you going to do?" Ann asked.

"I don't know. George is special to me, but he lives in a
different world. I keep thinking about how I feel about
him, but then I remember how wrong we are for each
other."

"Just because you had a fight? Everyone has fights.
Bob and I have fights, and we stay stupid things, but we
always make up."

While they were married, they fought surprisingly
little. What bothered Gail was more basic: the distance
between them, the distance built into their relationship.
And she didn't see how she could fix that. It would always
be hanging over their heads.

"When was the last time you had a boyfriend?" Ann
asked.

Gail didn't like the question and didn't see how it was
relevant. "I date," she simply said.

"How much since college? Not including Eddie. A
couple times?"

"Something like that." Gail's life was transparent. She
had never learned how to lie, and sometimes she wished
she had.

"Maybe it's not Eddie, then," Ann suggested, studying
Gail's face closely.

That comment rubbed Gail the wrong way. "What are you saying?" she intoned, firmly.

Ann shook her head. "Never mind. I was just curious."

Gail might not be the social butterfly, but she could smell bullshit when it was shoved in her face. "No you weren't. You were getting at something, and I want to know what it is." Gail could feel her temper leaking through.

"I didn't mean to upset you," Ann said.

"A little late for that now, isn't it?"

Ann set her face. "Maybe if you pushed Eddie like that, he would have told you what he needed."

"What do you know about it?"

"I know you haven't had a real relationship for years, maybe never, and you may not even know how."

A voice, timid and embarrassed, intruded. "Excuse me, Ma'am, may I help you?" Gail and Ann were next in line, and everyone was staring at them. So much for privacy.

Chapter Seventeen

By Thursday, Eddie had officially run out of food and alcohol. He had been drinking almost steadily since his parents left the cottage Sunday evening, camped out on the couch in front of the television with a large box of tissues and the curtains drawn. His stay had started as an overnighter. Since he didn't have anywhere to be Monday morning, he hadn't seen why he needed to travel home right away. But what had been true Sunday evening remained true Monday morning, and afternoon, and evening, and Tuesday, and Wednesday. Each day, he slept less and watched TV more, getting up only occasionally to fetch a snack from the kitchen or a fresh bottle from the liquor cabinet.

He awoke Thursday—he was sure it was Thursday, although he hadn't been keeping track—to the sound of a pounding at the front door, which was locked. He had turned off his cell phone, which didn't work very well at the cottage anyhow. And he had been ignoring phone calls on the cottage landline, letting them fall through to voicemail. But he couldn't ignore the incessant banging coming from the kitchen.

By the time he had shuffled to the front door, the

pounding had migrated from the room into his head,
which was throbbing in time to the beat being laid down
by the soon-to-be-dead man on the outside. Already angry
that he needed to dry out enough to make it to the liquor
store, now he had to deal with this.

Eddie unlocked the door and forced it open with a
scrape. "What the hell do you want?" Eddie's voice came
out in a hoarse, muffled groan. Eddie caught a glimpse of
Bob, before he realized the sunlight shining into the
kitchen, searing his retinas. He held up his hand to block
it.

Without a word, Bob forced his way into the kitchen.
He grabbed a tall glass from the shelf, filled it with cold
water from the spigot, held it out for Eddie, who took it.

"I'm not thirsty," Eddie said.

"Drink it!" Bob said. "Or else my voice gets louder."

Bob had made his point. Eddie took a sip.

"What are you doing here," Eddie asked, as Bob began
foraging through the refrigerator. "There's nothing left in
there."

Bob came up with a half-filled carton of eggs and
headed for the stove.

"Where'd those come from?"

"I just laid them myself. Now I'm going to cook them,
and you're going to eat."

"I'm not hungry," Eddie said.

"While I'm cooking, you can take a shower. You reek."

"Is this the way you treat Ann?" By now, Eddie was dealing with guilt over snapping at Bob when he first answered the door, but he was still searching for a way to express his frustration politely. He knew a socially accept-able reason why he shouldn't need to be polite, but his brain wasn't cuing him in on what it was. He saw no real-istic option but to give into Bob's orders, and maybe then Bob would leave him alone.

"No, this is not the way I treat Ann, because Ann doesn't disappear for days on end and drag me all the way out into the boonies to deal with her alcoholic binges." Bob's voice was steady, unemotional, matter-of-fact, but Eddie felt that he was ticked, bordering on pissed. That didn't make sense, somehow, but Eddie was in no condi-tion to figure it out.

He brought his glass of water upstairs, showered, shaved, brushed his teeth, changed, and actually felt a little better. Downstairs, the smell of scrambled eggs made him feel a little nauseous. But he sat at the table, where Bob had laid out a place setting with eggs and orange juice. Where did he get orange juice? And Eddie choked down a forkful of the springy yellow substance.

"I'm sorry," Bob said.

"Forget it," Eddie said. He never could hold a grudge.

"I mean, for all that stuff last weekend, with Gail and all."

"Oh, that." Eddie still wasn't ready to talk about Gail.

He would like to have believed that he hadn't even
thought of her since Sunday, but even he couldn't pretend
that wasn't true. Still, he needed to defuse the conversation. "You didn't do anything wrong. It wasn't your fault."

"Yeah, well, it still sucks." Bob sounded like a teenager
searching for words with which to talk about girls.

"What's so special about her?" Eddie found himself
asking anyhow, the question he didn't want answered,
didn't understand, and probably couldn't comprehend the
answer to. His voice felt angry as he said it.

"She's a long-term relationship. You don't have many
of those— *any* of those."

Indeed, Eddie didn't pursue long-term relationships.
He had never wanted one after Gail. He allowed himself
only one youthful indiscretion, and she was it. And she
still captivated his heart. Maybe she knew what she was
talking about: he didn't want to repeat their relationship.

"Do you want one of those?" Bob asked. "A long-term
relationship?"

Eddie moved to shake his head, but it only tilted. He
tried to say, "No," but instead it came out, "I don't know.
Maybe. But maybe she's right; we're doomed."

"You both were young, and you had a bad experience.
But that doesn't mean you're doomed."

Eddie's spirits lifted.

"What did she say?" Bob asked.

"She was pretty angry with me." Recalling the rage on

Gail's face struck Eddie in the heart anew. "She seemed pretty set against the idea. I mean, I get that. But it was so long ago. And you know me; normally it wouldn't even be an issue. But for some reason Gail holds a special place, right here." He hit his chest with his fist.

"Maybe you just never let her go, and that's why you never developed a relationship with anyone else."

Eddie didn't understand "never wanted to let her go," but the second part of Bob's theory fit. Ever since Gail, Eddie had lost interest in falling in love; really, truly falling in love— until she returned.

"It's unfair of Gail not to give you a chance," Bob said. "No matter what happened in the past, this is now."

Yeah, Eddie had said that.

"But," he continued, "you can't change the way she feels."

Eddie got that. He didn't like it, but he got it.

"You should probably find someone else to fall in love with."

Chapter Eighteen

*T*ime passed, and the days grew shorter, and the New England weather began to grow cold, and the leaves lost their green and fell from the trees, and life returned more or less to normal.

Ann threw Gail a surprise 30th birthday party, at work, on the company bill. The fact that she was paying for her own surprise birthday party, that didn't thrill her too much. She invited several of Gail's favorite clients, and Bob, and fortunately no George. She enjoyed spending time with the people on the guest list, but her 30th reminded her how old she was getting, and how little she had actually accomplished. Yes, she was a successful professional, but out of that list of accomplishments she had dreamed as a girl, so few of them she had actually achieved. She had wanted to do some traveling, maybe see Europe, had thought she would have had a husband and family, had already picked out names for her kids. She was going to write gripping stories about her adventures, like Jack London, but as it was, she only wrote professional articles and sales materials, and not that well. She was going to appear on the *Tonight Show*; so far, she hadn't even come close.

Meanwhile, Eddie had stopped going out as much as he used to, and he never threw parties anymore. He told himself what he also told everyone else, that he needed to slow down until the market picked back up. And that was true. But he knew the bigger reason was that he experienced no joy in it. If he had, he would have found the money. But as it was, he didn't feel like partying. He didn't feel like eating and drinking. He didn't feel like dancing. He didn't feel like dating or trolling for girls.

Instead, he spent a great deal of time browsing the world-wide web. He read about his industry, facts and opinions he had never heard before about the real-estate market. He discovered some tactics that were working for other agents, and he decided to try some of them for himself. He began to lose himself in online advertising and guerrilla marketing. He realized that the market had simply changed, and he took on a new mindset for a new market. He tried out Twitter and started a blog, even though he wasn't a writer. But he needed to occupy his time, and this is what excited him at the moment. He worked late into the morning, looking up from his laptop, through the delicate drapery on his living room window, to find the early morning sun illuminating the sky, silhouetting the half-bare, orange-yellow trees.

His Mom and Dad called occasionally, just to make sure that he was still alive and that his landlord hadn't thrown him out on his ear. He told them the same story he was telling anyone else who asked, that business was still slow, and that he was slowing down himself until things picked up again. He wondered if his parents thought the market crash to be a blessing in disguise because of that.

Eddie did not tell anyone about his online activities, not about any of the specifics, partly because he didn't want to jinx it and partly because it just felt too weird, too much unlike him.

He still didn't know what to do about Bob and Ann's dinner party. They had been planning it for several weeks, even mailed him an invitation, and he felt he owed them for their friendship. But he also didn't feel much like partying or even like socializing. He was in the midst of his own period of temptation, forty days and forty nights in the wilderness trying to find himself. But Eddie's 40 days had already stretched to several times that. The decision was made for him, however, when Bob left a message on Eddie's voicemail, reminding Eddie of the party and saying that they had already reserved a place for him.

So he went.

That's where he met Jennifer.

Every man has met Jennifer. Her name may not always be "Jennifer," but it's the same woman. She may not be dazzlingly beautiful—she may not even be his type. She is girl-next-door pretty, blonde, and buxom, and her voice sings with a gliding lilt that turns even the sturdiest man into mashed potatoes.

Eddie's Jennifer seized his attention from the moment he walked through the front door of Bob and Ann's flat. He saw that he was obviously in the middle of a setup, because Ann introduced them to each other, emitting that suspicious feeling a woman gives off when she has something up her sleeve. Either she didn't trust Eddie to find himself a respectable date, which was entirely reasonable, or she and Bob were worried about his recent hermit tendencies. Whichever it was, at the moment, he didn't care. He didn't even notice when Gail entered the room.

Gail also did not bring a date, and she would have had it no other way. She had even clarified to Ann that she was not interested in meeting anyone romantically. So Ann had promised to set her up with a gay guy she knew. Gail didn't know whether that was a bad joke, or whether Ann really did have a single, gay guest coming to the party.

The first thing Gail noticed was George drooling over an apple-cheeked blonde, fair-skinned, a delicate flower with boobs the size of Mount Rushmore. He laughed at what Gail was sure were stupid jokes. He held her drink for her.

"He sure bounced back fast," Gail muttered.

"What was that?" Ann asked.

"Nothing." But Gail was still glaring at Eddie.

"I hope that's okay," Ann said. "I know you have a history, but you're not involved, and so I introduced him to my brother's sister-in-law."

Gail took a second puzzling out that relationship, but she determined that the new girl must be Ann's brother's wife's sister, as if putting it that way made it any clearer. In any case, she was not just another one of the "bodies." She was probably for real, and from what Gail would observe that night, most definitely for real.

To be fair, Bob and Ann threw a good party. The kids were staying at Gramma and Grampa's, as usual, and besides the four of them and Jennifer, they had invited Gary, a gay accountant Ann knew, to sit next to Gail. Apparently it wasn't a joke. They also had invited the Jacobsens, a couple that Bob had met in his travels. Each guest had at least four others whom he had not previously met, which kept the discussion interesting. Bob made a wonderful party emcee. He drew everyone into the conversation, inducing each to share something about themselves. Gail didn't realize how much a people person he could be.

He kept calling her "successful," and Gail understood why, even though she still didn't feel "successful."

But in the end, all Gail remembered was that over those three hours, she learned more about Jennifer than she ever wanted to know. For example: Jennifer is the youngest of three siblings. She works as an elementary school teacher and hopes someday to have a big family. Gail couldn't even imagine wanting this woman anywhere near *her* kids. She loves French food, but she wishes she could cook herself. Despite her appreciation for fine cuisine, she couldn't boil water without step-by-step directions, and even then, she'd probably burn it. That was the one joke Gail actually found funny, probably a little too funny.

Still, as they all said their goodbyes, Gail made a special effort to shake George's hand and to tell him how happy she was for him.

This perplexed Eddie, because as far as he knew, he hadn't done anything that deserved congratulations. For a moment, he feared that she had run into him online and was outing him to his friends. So he smiled politely and said, "Thank you, and congratulations on your clinic." And he left for home.

———

On the way back to Gail's own apartment, she remembered how he had swept her off her feet, all those years ago. She recalled the moment with him on the beach at Ardor Point, and the sunset. She dwelled on the sadness of their relationship, that they couldn't make it work, and on how her chance with him was now completely gone, probably forever.

Chapter Nineteen

*G*ail and Ann had in fact been doing well, better than expected. But Ann still short-circuited company policy without discussing it first with Gail, which upset Gail every time it happened. In fact, Gail had been obsessing about it. They could have been doing so much better, instead of just depending on good luck, if only she had a partner who would abide by her business decisions. Gail was as flexible as the next person, and she always sought input, but when she set business policy, she expected it to be followed, because that was the only way she could control what her business actually did.

On this particular day, Gail finished up her last appointment of the day just in time to overhear Ann on the phone: "Don't worry about the bill. We'll work something out."

After Ann hung up, Gail marched over to behind Ann's desk, irked to the edge of her patience, hung over Ann's chair, looking over Ann's shoulder at the computer screen. "What was that all about?"

"That," Ann said, "was my client, and I've got it handled."

Gail straightened up, but didn't move from where she

was standing. Instead, she scowled down at her business partner, her blood pressure steadily rising. "What the hell do you think you're doing? ... How many times have we had this discussion already? ... You can't just go using business resources for your personal charity projects! ... How can you do this to me?! ... It's like I'm in business with Forrest Gump!"

"Yeah, but Forrest Gump was a millionaire." Even-tempered to the edge of tears.

"So not the point," Gail said.

"It's gotta be part of the point." Ann neither turned nor stood nor tried to escape. She didn't even try to look Gail in the eye.

"The point is that you're undermining everything I'm trying to do here!"

Finally, Ann spun around in her chair, stood at attention, pushed Gail out of the way. "Is this how you behave at your other clinic?" she shouted. "Like Ivan the Terrible?"

"No," Gail shot back. "At my other clinic, I actually fire disobedient employees!"

"But you can't fire me, can you?"

Saying that seemed to delight Ann, as a criminal might be delighted when he figures out that there's no evidence against him.

"Is that what's pissing you off?" Ann said. "I'm your partner. You're in it for the long haul. You can't fire a partner, and you made me your partner."

"I'm starting to think that was a bad move." Gail turned to leave, storming out.

Ann shouted after her, "You're doing just what you did to Eddie! You follow through on everything except relationships."

Gail slammed the door from the other side.

————

Next morning, Gail went into work a little later than usual, because she didn't have any appointments until late in the morning. Instead, she called Clarice at her Worcester clinic.

Clarice was excited to hear from her. But Gail cut short the hello's.

"How are things going there? Any interesting things happen in the clinic lately?"

Clarice told her an amusing story about a grouchy client who stormed out over a personality conflict with one of the clinic team— That is, it was *supposed* to be an amusing story. Gail didn't laugh, and she didn't understand how Clarice could possibly have laughed at it. Silliness, Clarice said, nothing they couldn't handle; it was just a bad match. Gail had always taught Clarice that they must fearlessly turn away the wrong clients in order to get the right ones. But Gail wondered whether, if she were there, she could have handled the situation better. She had worked hard to systematize almost everything she did there, but special situations would always arise that required the human touch. If she wasn't there, how would Clarice deal with them?

"I've been thinking of moving back," Gail said. That wasn't a complete lie, because the thought had indeed crossed her mind. But she had never actually considered it, seriously considered it, before mentioning it just then. Somehow, speaking it turned the fleeting thought into an actual possibility.

"Really?!" Clarice said. "Why?"

"I'm not sure I'm happy here," she heard herself say. She told Clarice about her summer weekend with George's family, about his new girlfriend, about her trouble with Ann, how Ann's last words to her had stung. Gail felt her life falling apart. And now she had discovered that they were experiencing problems, too.

But she couldn't just leave, because she had made a commitment to Ann. Besides, she didn't have enough money to start over yet again. Everything and everybody, just too close, closing in, trapped, like she wanted out but could barely breathe. And she had no one else to talk to.

"You still there?" Gail asked. Clarice had not said anything in too long.

"Yes, I'm still here. Still listening."

"Sometimes it's like I see myself going insane, like I'm looking at myself becoming a crazy person, but I can't do anything about it. Like this blonde George was with. I felt myself becoming jealous of her and thinking nasty things about her, and she's probably a wonderful person. And George deserves a wonderful person. What's wrong with me?"

"Maybe you just didn't expect him to get over you."

"Maybe." That theory made sense intellectually, but somehow it didn't ring true.

"Or, maybe... Maybe you still feel... uh."

"No," Gail said. "I can't go there."

"Can't go where?"

"I can't still have a thing for him. That was over and done with years ago."

"If you say so," Clarice said in that way that Gail knew meant, "Yeah, I don't believe you, not for an instant, but I can't change your mind if you're going to be that stubborn."

"Do you want to know what I think?" Clarice continued.

"No, but tell me anyhow," Gail said, thinking she would remind her again of her non-existent love life. For as long as Gail had known Clarice, she had not dated, had actively resisted dating, had remained uninterested in men. There was even a rumor at one point that she might be a lesbian, or a nun, or something. And it was only through the stories of her marriage, plus the occasional casual date, that Gail was able to set the record straight.

"I think you're looking for an excuse to get out," Clarice

said. "Now, I don't know if it's because your ex is there, or whether there's something wrong with your business partner there, or what, because I'm not there, and I don't know them. But there's nothing here that really requires your personal attention. I mean, yeah, we'd love to see you. But you shouldn't use that as an excuse to do something you'll regret. Maybe if you stick with it, it'll get better. Things weren't always so fun here, either, if you remember."

True enough. Even after Gail got over the initial panic, that something might go wrong and she might end up broke and homeless, she still made some hard decisions. The first time she had to fire someone, the experience left her hyperventilating and retching over the toilet. But she didn't leave. She stuck with it until it worked.

"You follow through on everything except relationships," Ann had shouted at her. Ann's anger had been shouting, Gail knew. They could make up. And Gail did follow through on relationships. She knew she did. But she didn't appreciate being forced to stick with a bad situation just because it would look like she was giving up otherwise. Sometimes, you gotta know when to cut loose, she thought.

"What you should do," Clarice said, "is to find someone there you can trust, you can talk to, who knows your business partner and the dynamics involved, and ask them whether they think it's worth salvaging. Even if they can't connect the dots for you, they might at least be able to help you find out where the dots are."

Unfortunately, she could think of only one name, only one person who fit that description, who she could trust with talk about Ann, who she knew would at least listen to her without judging her.

———

Eddie's head was reeling from his first officialdate with Jennifer. The date itself was nothing all that impressive. They went out to dinner, appreciated the food, made fun of the waiter, talked about their pasts, presents, and futures. They actually covered quite a lot of ground.

But it had been a long time since anyone made him feel quite like this, connected, central to being, as though she could be the reason he was placed on this world. Something about her took him over, something in the way she talked to him, something in the way she looked at him, maybe even something in what she said, though Eddie was so infatuated that he would have swooned at her rendition of "Twinkle Twinkle Little Star," would have called it original and inspiring, a work of art.

Eddie recognized the feeling. And he saw now what he had been doing with it all these years, pushing it off and throwing it away like yesterday's smelly garbage. Even that first night, after he had first met Jennifer, he had found himself falling into those familiar thought patterns, pushing off the thoughts he had been thinking about her.

But now, Eddie was ready to act.

Eddie was falling in love.

And he was through running away from it. He hadn't even realized that he was doing so, but now, looking back, what could he conclude except that all those years, he had been running. He had always kept relationships casual or nothing. He would never have allowed himself to fall this far this fast for anyone, not since he was a teenager.

He drove Jennifer to her apartment, and she invited him up for a nightcap. The place was neatly but sparsely furnished, a roomy kitchen area but with very little counter space; plush, beige carpeting everywhere else, as far as the eye could see; a comfy looking white leather couch, and a glass coffee table; opposite it, a solitary wide-screen TV, lonely, mounted to the wall.

He could tell that she didn't care much for décor as a subject area, probably not any more than she cared about cooking. He could work with that. Between the two of them, they could live together tastefully and comfortably.

Without a word, she turned, dropped her keys on the coffee table, and grabbed him by the ears, pulling his lips to hers. He returned the favor and kissed her and held her, caressing her face with one hand, reaching with the other under her coat and along the sleek fabric of her evening dress. But the kiss was surprisingly anticlimactic, not electric as he had expected. Rather, he felt merely close, comfortable, happy, as though he were a part of her, and she of him. Oneness.

"I'm falling in love with you," he whispered into her
ear, expecting her either to blush or to freak out that it
was going too fast, or maybe to think he was joking.

Instead, she backed up a step, horror showing in her
eyes. "I'm sorry," she said. "I thought we were just having
a good time. A little fun. Nothing serious."

He knew the speech by heart. He had performed it
himself numerous times. And he always thought he had
done a good rendition of it, letting the girl down easily,
whoever she might be. Now he realized, there was no such
thing. "Letting her down easy" was just a euphemism for
"making myself feel better for being a cad."

"I see," he said, and before she could say another word,
"I know the speech by heart. And I deserve it, believe me,
because I've used it plenty of times myself. Maybe we
could just call it a night, then. No hard feelings?"

She nodded in agreement. "No hard feelings. I'm
sorry."

"I know," he said, and he kissed Jennifer on the cheek,
lightly, before turning and sauntering away in a face-
saving gait, never to return.

Chapter Twenty

*E*ddie dragged himself through the front door of his home, visually surveyed his mail, sitting on the floor under the mail slot since it had arrived earlier that day. One blank envelope no doubt contained a credit-card offer, which would surely be turned down if he were to bother to send in the application. He didn't feel like being rejected any more right now. A bill from the cable company protruded from the pile. At this rate, he would be living without cable pretty soon, because he was out of money, having just spent the last of it on a date that ended in suffering, followed by just enough gasoline to get home tonight and back to the office in the morning. After that, he didn't know what he was going to do for trans-portation.

He started by opening the blank envelope, which turned out not to be a credit-card offer. Rather, it contained notice of a bounced-check, with a $55 penalty. So now his account was overdrawn by $55 more than it had been previously.

"Wonderful," he said sarcastically to himself, or maybe to God.

At least they weren't foreclosing on his house... yet.

But he was on the verge of defaulting. Eddie didn't think he could stand that. With the trickle of commissions he was able to get, he was just barely keeping his head above water.

None of his marketing efforts had paid off yet, not in any significant way. But at least they had kept him from descending into depression. Trying anything was better than doing nothing, even though it sometimes upset him how little progress he had made.

But tonight, he didn't want to try anything, didn't want to be connected online, didn't want acceptance or rejection. He just really wanted a drink, and unfortunately he was out of alcohol, and he was skint, and that, as they say, was that.

He lay on the couch, turned on the TV, switched to a romantic movie he had never seen before, got lost in someone else's problems for a change, ached, cried a little, finally fell asleep.

———

It was about a year after the divorce that I finally got over Gail. I had bought a house in Hull, got a real-estate license, and entered the booming real-estate market. Those were lucrative times, with lots of money, lots of fun, lots of friends, and eventually lots of sex.

That's when I took on the name "Eddie," not by choice. A smart aleck by the name of Elton Kerry forced the name on me against my will. He said "George" was too stuffy, and so he started calling me "Eddie."

If you've never had yourself renamed, let me tell you, it's awkward. It feels wrong. And when everyone starts calling you the wrong name, and you don't respond to them, they think you're ignoring them or you're hard of hearing or something. That's pretty awkward, too.

But my friends really seemed to enjoy calling me "Eddie." For their sake, I gave them a choice, responding to both names, because I wanted them to like me. Eventually, however, "George" faded out of use, except for my parents, and I even introduced myself as "Eddie." The transformation was complete.

———

Gail sat on the couch of her apartment, lonely and alone, feeling guilty for having lost her temper with Ann. She debated what to do the following morning. Call in sick? Cancel her appointments? She literally feared to go into the office, because she expected to end up in another fight.

She still felt the sting of Ann's last words to her. She couldn't get them out of her mind. Some part of her suspected that Ann had chosen them to have maximum lethal effect. "You always give up on relationships, don't you?" That's not what Ann had said, but that's what Gail heard now in her mind. What hurt Gail wasn't just that Ann thought this of her. What hurt Gail was the feeling that Ann was onto something, that she actually had a good reason to have said such a cruel thing, that she had

evidence, names, dates, places, and bodies, facts at her
fingertips, ready to throw them at Gail if she tried to
defend herself.

But even through betrayal, Ann was her friend. And
friends forgive friends, don't they?

The business in Worcester, Gail couldn't bear the
thought that they didn't need her there. Intellectually,
rationally, she knew that Clarice was more than capable.
Gail had trained her well, and she was more than just an
employee: Clarice had a passion for the business. Gail's
biggest fear was that Clarice would leave to start her own
business. But until then, the Worcester clinic was in good
hands.

And that made Gail useless. No surprise there,
because uselessness is why she had left for more exciting
adventures in the first place. So why, then, did she long to
return? To return to boring, to useless, to rote, when she
was the creative genius, the adventurer, the entre-
preneur?

Truthfully, if she left the business in Waltham now, it
would probably survive. If something—God forbid—were
to happen to her unexpectedly, Ann and Bob would probably be able to hire someone to help out and make a go at
it. George would probably throw in some help, too, probably more time and effort than even Bob would, for Ann's
business.

Gail groaned at the thought, that George would give of

himself so readily and so fully to keep her business going, even after her hypothetical demise. Uselessness felt like hopelessness and failure, because all of the purpose in her life she had bound up in her now-useless career.

She knew how she had left it with George, that they weren't even friends anymore, just rare acquaintances. But alone and lonely, she wanted to hear his voice, because he was the one person who had always listened. He didn't always hear her, but he always listened, and he always cared.

She picked up the phone and called him at home. By that time, it was late, after one in the morning. Before the phone stopped ringing, she feared that she might wake him. Or even worse, that she might interrupt a romantic escapade.

He answered, groggy.

"George, it's me, Gail. I'm sorry for waking you, but I just really needed to talk to someone who cares. And for all of our problems together, you still always cared, and I was hoping, maybe, you could talk to me for a while?"

———

Gail's call moved Eddie's heart. She sounded on the verge of tears. He suggested that he meet her somewhere. Therefore, he drove all the way in to Gail's place, almost an hour's drive, just because she had called. He knew it would use up the last of the gasoline in his tank, and he didn't know how he was going to get back home again, but he would find a way. Maybe he could bum a ride to the office and stay there until morning. He'd done it before. He didn't know how he would then get back to his car, or what he would do with it once he managed that. But he couldn't figure out everything just then. She needed him, and in a way, Eddie needed her at that particular moment, because he needed her to need him.

He found her building easily enough, his car running on fumes. He rang at the front door, which buzzed to let him in. By the time he reached her apartment inside, she was waiting for him, and he could see that she had been crying. Without a word, he took her up into his arms and held her, rubbed her stiffened neck, kissed her through her mussed curls, not as a sexual overture, but as an act of love and companionship. He knew she needed his friendship, and for the first time since they had reen-countered each other, possibly for the first time ever, he was able to give it to her.

Gail was tearing up again. It felt so good to be held, and she didn't care anymore whether he had ulterior motives or not. She wondered whether she was now a temptation to him, or how his new girlfriend would feel about him coming to see her. But she needed someone to reach out to, and she was desperate.

She broke the embrace and wiped her eyes. "I'm sorry I got you over here. I don't even know why I called you."

"Because you were upset and you needed someone to

talk to," he answered for her.

"But what would Jennifer think of you coming over here?" Surely, Jennifer didn't know. After all, Gail reasoned, if it had been *her* boyfriend who wanted to go see his ex-wife in the middle of the night, alone, for any reason, she would have had a big problem with that.

"There's nothing between Jennifer and me," Eddie said.

"But at Bob and Ann's party." She shook her head. "I'm sorry. It just looked like there was something there."

She deserved an explanation, so Eddie did the best he could without going into details. "There was, but it didn't work out."

Gail was on the roller-coaster again, because George was back in her life, and unattached, and probably obsessed with her. "So what does that mean? For us? I don't know that I want to go through this again."

"I'm sorry I got out of control before," Eddie said.

"You know," Eddie chuckled, "I didn't think I could ever fall in love again with anyone else besides you, but now, I know that I can, and I will. Gail, you'll always have a special place in my heart, and that won't ever change, because you were a special part of my life. But if you need a friend, I'm here for you now."

Gail was choking up amidst a flood of mixed emotions. "Thank you," she managed.

"What happened?" Eddie asked, ushering her to a

chair.

"I don't know. Everything. Too much." Where to start?

"Does it have anything to do with me?"

She shook her head, no. "I don't know." She shrugged. "Maybe."

"Maybe you should start at the beginning."

"I just feel so overwhelmed. I don't know where I'm going anymore."

He felt bad about not being there for her during all that time. "And I pressured you," he said, "and alienated you, just when you needed someone. And I realize now why that wigged you out, and I shouldn't have done that. I'm sorry."

In a way, their relationship was now more like that of a brother and sister than of lovers. As an only child, Eddie had never had a sister, and he wasn't quite sure how he was supposed to feel or behave. But it felt right having Gail as a sister, because he loved her deeply, and that was a way for him to express his love.

"Thank you," she said. "But it's not about that."

"Okay, so then why don't I make us some tea, and you can fill me in."

Eddie put on the kettle while they talked, made each a much-too-hot cup of the dark infusion, each on a saucer, which each held as they settled onto the couch. Meanwhile, phrase by phrase, exchange by exchange, Gail managed to sketch a picture of how she felt about her work, her confusion, her emptiness.

Eddie had never experienced exactly what she was going through, but at least he understood why she felt so overwhelmed.

She finally got to the part about Ann's hurtful words, that she always gave up on the people in her life, just like she had given up on him, capping off the sentiment with an exasperated "Do you believe that?"

"Well," Eddie said carefully but casually, "in a way, maybe she's right—" He quickly backpedaled, even before noticing whatever reaction she might have had. "It's not your fault," he said. "Neither one of us, I think, really saw it through, one way or the other. But that's the way life is sometimes. It doesn't mean there's anything wrong with you. And it doesn't mean you can't change your direction, if you're not happy with it the way it is. I mean, look at me. I thought my life was over. I didn't think I could ever fall in love again, but then I did."

He felt an almost Zen peace about the subject. Maybe because of endorphins, maybe because of the company, maybe because of the tea. For whatever reason, he saw that he had been both loved and rejected, and he had survived.

"You're talking about Jennifer?" Gail asked. For once, she didn't feel envy at having spoken the name, and she felt a little sorry for George.

He nodded. "Today, I discovered what it feels like to

fall in love and to have my heart broken, all in one fell swoop. I've done that to so many women before, but I never knew what it felt like." He shook his head. "I would have asked her to marry me, you know. I was ready."

"Well, you were never one to go slow," she said.

She always admired about him his love of life. He didn't always go all the way to the goal. Sometimes, he didn't even know where the goal was. But as far as he went, wherever he went, he always plunged in and enjoyed himself getting there.

"We're just a couple of sorry, old halfwits," Gail said, and she settled into his bosom as she sipped her tea.

"Speak for yourself!" Eddie said.

Gail giggled. She was feeling better already.

Chapter Twenty-One

*G*ail knew what would make her feel better, or at least what would help her to think better. But it was a crazy idea. The ultimate crazy. So that's where she started in broaching the subject.

"You want to do something crazy?"

Crazy was not in Gail's character. She lived the opposite of crazy. She stood for plans, stability, organization, follow-through. All those years, Eddie had begged her to get crazy, and now, when he couldn't afford it and probably couldn't handle it, now she wants to do something crazy.

"I thought you had the crazy gene surgically removed at birth," he said.

"Well, there's actually a logic behind it."

"I can't afford any crazy right now." He felt his face go hot. "Sorry."

"You don't even know what I have in mind!"

"Okay. I'll hear you out. *Then* I'll explain why I can't."

"Well, as long as you have an open mind." She gulped down the last of her tea.

"What is it?" he asked, now curious.

She sat up, turned and faced him. "Do you have

anywhere to be tomorrow?"

"No," he said. "Just work. Not real work; check my messages, update my listings, that sort of thing." He carefully left out any details, including the fact that he didn't know if he could even make it to the office, because his car had been scolding him, "Fuel empty!" on the way over.

"Let's drive up to your parents' cottage at Ardor Point."

It was practically winter. Yes, some of the autumn leaves were still hanging onto their branches, but they were doing so out of sheer desperation, not because they actually belonged there.

"It's really cold up there," he said, again not wanting to get into the details of his real problem, which was that he likely as not couldn't make it to a gas station, never mind the two-and-a-half-hour trip to Maine.

"Doesn't the cottage have a fireplace?"

"Yes, but—" There was no doubt wood available for the fireplace, but the kitchen would be bare, and the water would be turned off for the winter, and they would need to at least buy breakfast, and he had no money for that either.

"You can get in, right? You have the key?"

"Yes..." Even if he didn't have the key, he knew where the spare was hidden.

"So then let's go. It'll be fun."

He stared at her, bewildered. She actually seemed excited to up and drop everything and shuttle away to the bitter cold.

"Why?" he asked. "Why a frozen, barren cottage? Why at three-thirty in the morning?"

"Because I want to see the sun come up, and if we leave now, we might just be able to make it in time."

"Don't you have appointments tomorrow? How are you going to get back to work?"

"I'll call Ann and have her cancel or reschedule my appointments. I never call in sick, and I deserve a little leeway."

Eddie couldn't believe his ears. He reached out and felt her forehead.

She shot him back a funny look. "What's that all about."

"Just making sure you don't have a fever."

Sober, "I know it sounds whacked, but I'm really serious. I think being there will help me think better. And you still owe me a ride on the Laser."

"I think Dad's probably packed it up for the season."

"Fine, but we still need to make sure you can stand me there, so I can come out when the weather warms up again."

He knew he had lost, or would lose soon, and he wasn't completely disappointed by it. He mentally prepared for the next thing he had to say.

Gail stared at him with puppy-dog eyes and said, "Please."

"Two points," he said. "I have no gas in my car, so we have to take yours."

"Fine," she said.

"And..." His face flushed again. "I have no money in my checking account, so you have to buy us breakfast, or else we'll starve to death."

"That's it? No problem. Let's go."

She didn't even seem to notice his discomfort, but in reality she had realized how important it was for him to treat her, rather than the other way around. She made as little fuss about it as she could, so that he wouldn't feel too bad about it. At the same time, she thought, it's about time that she got a chance to do something nice for him, rather than the other way around.

———

Once Gail was behind the wheel, steering the only pair of headlights on the highway, rock radio beating softly in the background as they rolled forward at slightly-faster-than-the-speed-limit, "Why did you get married, if you didn't want a commitment until now?"

Eddie puzzled over the question. Had he gotten married and no one told him about it? But instead of making a wisecrack, as he was thinking, he merely said, "I don't understand. What do you mean?"

"If you just now decided you were ready for a relation-ship, why did you marry me ten years ago?" She wanted to know how much she was at fault for their breakup, but she knew that if she just asked him straight out, he would take all the blame, leaving her no wiser off than when she started.

"Has it been ten years?" he said.

"Almost. Do you think that was one reason why we didn't work out?"

"I did want a commitment back then, but... I think what happened is that after we broke up, I never truly got over you."

His voice was steady, but Gail could still see that special place he had reserved for memories of her inside his psyche.

"Until recently." He finished the thought.

The truth struck into her heart, that he probably would have stayed with her, happily playing second fiddle to her first, if she hadn't mentioned "divorce." She probably could have convinced him to move to Worcester with her, if she had tried. She wasn't convinced that would have been better.

Eddie asked the next obvious question. "Why didn't you ever remarry?"

"Because my whole life was taken up with my work. I just didn't have anything left over for a relationship."

"That's one thing I always respected you for," Eddie said, "that you knew what you wanted, and you kept at it until you got it. Steady, no waffling. No matter what else happened between us, I always admired you for that."

"So what do I want now then?"

"I don't know. Do you think that's why you feel... 'empty'? Is that the word you used?"

She nodded without looking at him, easy with the excuse that she needed to keep her eyes on the road.

While she didn't know what she was looking for, she did think that if she found it, it would fill her life again and give her purpose. For whatever reason—whether because of lack of sleep, or because of the feeling of rebelliousness, or because of the person she was with—at that moment, driving through the dark to a fool's destination, for no good reason except that she wanted to, it all enthused, inspired, and gladdened her.

———

From the Holtzman's dock, Gail could see the sun peeking through the trees of Birch Island, sending yellow light streaming across the water. Even though the dock itself had been taken in for the winter, George showed her the perfect spot from which to view the rising sun.

Eddie stood shivering next to her. He had bundled up in his winter coat, teeth chattering in the chilled, gusty air. Meanwhile, Gail looked warm and toasty, the ends of her lips curving upward, despite her rosy cheeks, windswept hair, and the fact that she was wearing only a brown leather jacket over her blouse.

"You look happy," he said.

"I think I am."

"What is it about this place that makes you happy?"

Something about the infinity of the wide open skyline, the smell of the sea wind, the sand shifting beneath her feet, the clear sun and sky, just helped clear her mind, relaxed her. If she only stayed here long enough, all of the fragments would come together, and she could become a whole person.

Standing out there on the beach, she began to talk, to emptied herself of the confusion and complexity, in a single stream of consciousness. Between shivers and chittering teeth, Eddie nodded and understood. He didn't say much, just listened, and Gail's needs started to make sense to her, and her desires started to fall into place.

They eventually made it back to the abandoned cottage, where Eddie prepared them some hot cocoa, one of the few items that littered the now mostly bare kitchen shelves and cupboards, using a little spring water that had been left in the refrigerator. He had already built a fire in the fireplace, and Gail pushed the couch up close to it, to warm herself from the general chill. She called Ann at the office and left her a voicemail that she wasn't feeling well, asking Ann to please take or reschedule her day's appointments. Gail had never called in sick and was rarely even late, and she reasoned, uncharacteristically, that she was due.

Maybe she was experiencing some sort of spiritual awakening. Or madness. Or maybe both. Pushing off the

uselessness of work, because she had finally had enough?
Is this what going crazy feels like?

Eddie brought in the hot cocoa, a large mug in each
hand, and handed one to Gail. She wrapped her delicate
fingers around it, letting them soak in the warmth. The
sight stirred up a familiar pang in Eddie's heart, but he
quickly redirected it. Gail would always hold a special
place in his heart, but there was nothing romantic
between them.

"I'm a nice person, aren't I?" Gail asked.

"Yes, absolutely," Eddie said.

"Then why don't people like me?"

"I don't understand. People like you fine. I don't know
anyone who doesn't like you."

Gail often felt disliked, unloved, and especially of late.
She searched for someone to pose as an example. "What
about your mother."

"She likes you. I think she just needs to get used to the
fact that we aren't married anymore." Eddie thought of
his own struggle with that very truth, a struggle which
even then he had not completely overcome, but at least he
saw the light.

"So why do I always seem to have such trouble with
relationships?"

"I don't know." Eddie's own past served as an object
lesson. "Maybe we all sometimes push people away, probably the people we need the most."

To Gail, that sounded like an accusation. "What's that supposed to mean?"

"Nothing. I was just thinking of how I've pushed away anyone who might have snapped me out of the valley I was in." He continued in that vein, opening up his soul to her.

"I've never told anyone this," he finally said. "I'm out of money, completely skint, broke, bankrupt, nothing left. I've been running out ever since the crash, and I've been avoiding it rather than dealing with it."

He told her about his more recent efforts, how they gave him hope, but that nothing had paid off. He revealed his discouragement. He revealed his loneliness, told her sometimes he was afraid people would wouldn't love him if he couldn't buy their love, told her about all the women he pushed away that could have been a companion to him, and the women he attached himself to, because he knew they would never require anything of him except sex. He even told her about Shara the psychiatrist, and the kiss, and his guilt, and that he had hid it from her all these years because he didn't want to hurt her, and that he was only telling her now because he thought she deserved to know. She seemed to take the story in stride, as though it were no more disturbing than a report on the weather.

And he found himself telling her that maybe it was the hard things in a relationship that made it worth having, that maybe it was all the fighting and the bad feelings, that if you could get through those, maybe then you have something worth keeping.

He had been babbling, but Gail didn't seem to mind. She even threw in stories of her own. She told him about the dates that she had had, boring stories that were hardly worth telling. She could count them on the fingers of one hand. She told him about her father, his love of discipline, that he seemed always at odds with her brother growing up, but that she was his pride and joy, and how he had instilled in her what would become a love for her work. And how she felt sorry for her brother because of his speech disability. She explained that's why she had gone into her chosen field, and she told him stories of the kids that she had helped and how good it made her feel. But while she had always been dedicated to her work, she had failed when it came to the people in her life.

Eddie had of course heard some of these stories before, but he didn't mind hearing them again, if she wanted to tell them.

As they continued to talk through the early morning hours, the heat radiating onto their arms and faces, the wood smog permeating the room, they eventually grew tired. She reclined onto his chest and closed her eyes and continued to listen and to talk. He stroked her hair and continued to listen and to talk.

Eddie dreamed about Gail.

Chapter Twenty-Two

We are back at Basilio's, as my dream begins. I help Gail on with her coat, and I tell her we should do this again sometime. She agrees, and seems genuinely happy. I open the car door for her and lean over and kiss her. She kisses me back, a deep, connected kiss. She wraps her arms around me, pulling me to herself. I am fast falling in love with her, and although I feel uncomfortable about it, I'm excited and enjoying it, like nothing I have ever experienced. I tell her as much, then we're in her apartment.

She becomes angry with me, and my heart feels like it's going to explode. I plead with her, tears rolling down my cheeks: please reconsider. I tell her how much I need her, that she is the love of my life, that I'll never be anything without her. But she is offended that I would even suggest such a ludicrous idea. I mean nothing to her. I was just a phase in her life, a foolish, youthful indiscretion.

And then she throws "that woman" in my face. I know she means Shara, a woman I met one night in a bar during a particularly lonely time when we were married. Shara appears wearing a tiny, black dress, wooing me with her sultry, smoky voice. And then I remember that I had already told Gail about Shara, and she seemed okay that we had slept together, but now she's upset with me.

(In real life, Shara and I never slept together, but in my dream, I believe that we had, and that's what Gail is upset about.)

But I ignore Shara, hoping she'll go away, and tell Gail that she had said she was okay with it, that it was all in the past. I tell Gail that her forgiveness means more than anything else she has ever done for me. I beg her not to change her mind about that. I tell her again that she is the only woman for me, that no other woman I've ever slept with meant anything to me, including Shara.

I awake, feeling desolate, with Gail actually in my arms, as we had fallen asleep on the couch in front of the fire. The fire has dwindled, and the temperature is dropping again. But I just want to hold her close, and I wonder whether I should tell her about the dream. I wonder what it means, or whether it means anything at all.

———

They awoke in each other's arms. Eddie was reclining against the couch armrest, and Gail had snuggled up in his bosom. They couldn't have been sleeping for more than a few hours, because the fire was still burning, though barely. But even though the air in the room was quickly cooling, Eddie didn't want to get up in order to stir the fire, put another log on. Instead, all he wanted to do was to hold Gail. He put his arm around her, and he bent down and kissed her on the top of her head.

She opened her eyes and stared up at George. She cuddled in his warmth. She wondered if he might be feeling affections for her again, but this time, without anxiety. She didn't know why he loved her, but he obviously did, had dropped everything and driven half-way to Canada in the middle of the night, simply because she had asked him to. He was either crazy or devoted, and she was convinced he wasn't crazy. She was beginning to wonder why she had been such a fool, because she had possessed a wonderful man, and she had thrown him away.

Gail could see the upset in George's expression, his face pained, his lips sad. "What's wrong?"

He riffled his fingers over her hair and massaged her neck. "Nothing," he said. "I just had a bad dream."

"I'm sorry," she said coquettishly. And before she knew what she was doing, she had taken advantage of her superior position, had slithered up George's body, and was kissing him passionately, rubbing her way down his torso with her hand. She slid her tongue past his lips, as his eyes bulged in surprise.

At first, Eddie eased into Gail's presence, even the feeling of her body pressed up against his. But when he realized she was making a sexual overture, he caught himself and pushed her away. He stood and breathed deeply to steady his nerves.

"What are you doing?" he said. Those weren't the right words. They didn't feel right. "I mean, where are you going with this?" That wasn't it, either.

"I don't know," she said, flustered.

He stood about three feet from her, looked her straight in the eye, and said, "Do you want to get back together again?" It came out sounding like he was asking her to rob a bank with him.

She could hardly believe she was thinking what she was thinking, but there was no denying it. "Yes," she said, and her lips sealed shut.

"Are you sure?" he said. "Because if you change your mind... I just don't think I could handle that."

She understood exactly what he meant, and her understanding pressed down on her shoulders like a yoke. He was not just after something fun; he was after something serious. And if she broke up with him again, she would not just sadden him; she would devastate him. But she finally knew what she wanted, and for her, George was the best person with whom to meet that challenge.

She nodded. "I'm sure."

He stopped a moment to consider her. He was never one for playing it safe in any case. "Okay," he said. "Let's do it."

They kissed, and he took her hand and led her down to the floor before the dwindling fire. To Gail, it was just a

continuation of the last great time they made love, as if
they had never stopped being one flesh. They had only
taken a brief hiatus in their relationship, but they had
always been inextricably linked, inextricably one.

When they were finished, they lay next to each other,
Gail's head on George's arm. Gail rolled over to gaze at
the profile of George's nose, the straight bridge on which
his glasses usually sat, his eyes, thin lips, the fur on his
lip, blazing a path down his sturdy chin. Her face lit up as
she ran a finger through the straight hair on his chest.

"Should I call you 'Eddie'?" she said. "Or would you
prefer I keep calling you 'George'?"

He kissed her forehead. "You can call me anything you
want."

"Yeah, but what do you *want* me to call you?"

He considered the question for a moment. "I think I'd
like *you* to call me 'George.'"

———

Later that afternoon, Gail drove them both back to her
apartment. She forced a few $20's on George, saying, "Get
some gasoline. I'll follow you to the gas station to make
sure you make it there okay."

When George hesitated, she shoved the money into his
pocket. "You helped me out when I was going through
school, and I would never have been able to make it
without you. So now it's my turn to help you out until you
get back on your feet." Without missing a beat, "Can we

spend the night together again tonight?"

George leaned over and kissed her. "Your place or
mine?"

"I wanted to talk to Ann," she said, worrying as she
had earlier that Ann might not have gotten her message,
might not have rescheduled her appointments. "After
that, we can do whatever you'd like."

"I should check in at the office for messages and email.
We can meet back here afterward and decide. How's
that?"

"Wonderful," Gail said, grinning.

He kissed her again, said goodbye, and jumped into his
car, which made it to the gas station with fumes to spare.
And there was Gail, pulling in behind him. Apparently,
she decided to fill up her car, too.

A full tank and a few flirtatious waves later, George
said, "Why don't you call me on my cell when you're on
your way back? Then I can meet you at your place."

She nodded, and they were off, Gail to find Ann, and
George to visit his office.

————

George sifted through a stack of emails and several voice-
mails, but little of interest, until he got to an email from
David Richardson, whom he had met online and to whom
he had been giving advice on his blog about what to watch
for in buying a fixer-upper. The email was to ask him
about a property he had listed and linked to from his

website.

Eddie looked up the property, an old house that its owners were desperate to unload. He replied with some general information and said he could set up an appointment for David and his wife Devon to see the old house. But he had low hopes of anything significant coming from this email, because he simply didn't expect a fixer-upper to be right for the Richardsons, and he did expect them to figure that out soon enough. Chances were, they were looking at this house because they simply weren't ready to buy, and they didn't realize that a fixer-upper can cost as much to fix up as a proper house would cost to buy.

Eddie took a moment, before he hit the "send" button, a moment to wonder if he was completely washed up. Maybe he should just call it a career, and look for something else, something he'd be better at.

———

Gail stopped by the office, even though it was a little late in the day, and found the suite empty. Still, she checked her messages and calendar. It appeared that Ann had indeed cleared Gail's schedule for the day and had rescheduled the appointments. Gail would need to remember to thank her for that, even though she hadn't called back to confirm. Gail understood why her business partner might not want to have talked with her that particular day, considering the circumstances. She was beginning to feel guilty; she would have to remember to

doubly thank Ann for taking care of business while she
was gone, and hope that Ann would forgive her for taking
off on such an escapade, with no notice whatsoever.

She made a few phone calls. Ann's cell rang through to
voicemail, and Gail left a message asking her to please
call back so that they could talk and she could apologize.
Trying different numbers, she finally got in touch with a
human being: Bob, at his office. Gail told him she was
trying to get in touch with Ann and was concerned about
her, because she wanted to make sure everything was
okay. Bob explained that Ann was still upset, but that as
far as he knew, she went into work for the day.

Finally, Gail hopped back in her car and drove to Ann's
house. Ann's car sat in the driveway, but Gail had to ring
the bell five times before her partner answered, a frown
covering her face.

The first words out of Gail's mouth were, "I'm sorry."

"I'm sorry, too," Ann said. She was still dressed for
work, in dark slacks and a delicate, powder blue blouse.
The cold air blew through the doorway and into the foyer,
and Ann huddled up inside her own arms, shivering and
trying to keep warm.

"May I come in?" Gail asked. "We can get out of this
cold."

"Sure," Ann said, still frowning, and silently allowed
Gail to enter.

Two small boys ran past, and Ann stopped them a

moment and asked them to play in their room for a few
minutes, "so Mommy can have an *important meeting*."
Soberly, they agreed and dashed off. Gail realized how
little she knew about her partner's life outside of work,
and the things that must have been ultimately important
to her.

Once they had settled on Ann's linen-colored couch,
Gail prepared to begin her speech, but before she could,
Ann started hers.

"I don't know whether this is going to work."

"What?" Gail asked.

"This partnership. Maybe you were right. Maybe it was
a bad idea from the start."

That was the last thing Gail expected to hear, and the
last thing she wanted to hear. So she did her best to get
her two cents in before the situation completely fell apart.
"Ann, what you said to me really hurt—"

"I know," Ann said, ashamed. "I'm sorry."

"But you were right." Gail felt tears bubbling into her
sinuses.

Ann shook her head, touching Gail's shoulder. "No,
hon. I shouldn't have said it."

"I don't know," Gail said, holding in the sobs, "whether
it will work, either. But I think we need to carry it
through to the end. We need to try everything we can to
make it work."

Ann wrestled with Gail's words for a moment. She

handed Gail a box of tissues from the table. "Okay, but..."
Ann struggled.

"I have to let you have your way sometimes and stop
trying to pretend I'm the only one in charge." Gail sniffed
and dabbed at her eyes.

Ann smiled. "I wouldn't put it that way."

But Gail was ready to put it just that way. She said
she was through sacrificing relationships for other priorities. Ann had been right, that Gail was empty, had been
feeling empty, and she needed to make a change. She told
Ann all about her night with George, and that they were
now back together again.

"I know he had dated Jennifer," Gail explained, "but he
said they broke up, if they were even actually going
together." That was close enough to what George had told
her, close enough for Ann's information. "I don't actually
know what was happening there."

"My brother says she's a 'wild woman,'" Ann said, "to
her face no less." She rolled her eyes. "I figured Eddie was
the safest one to pair her up with. I think she's young and
hasn't settled down yet, that's all."

"Isn't she our age?" Gail asked.

"In her twenties."

"I was in my twenties just a couple weeks ago."

Ann shook her head. "She's more 'in her twenties' than
you ever were, even when you actually were in your twenties."

Gail didn't like to be reminded of how little she had accomplished in her life. "Ouch!"

"No! I didn't mean it that way."

Gail suspected that Ann didn't actually know what had caused her to react.

"I just mean," Ann said, "that you've always been mature. I don't think I've ever known you to be flighty. I've never known you when you weren't putting your mind to something, and succeeding at it."

"So, do you think we can make this partnership work?"

Ann paused for moment, then nodded, slowly at first. "Yes, I think so. I hope so."

"Do you think that I can make it work with George?"

"I don't know," Ann said.

"He said that if we broke up again, he wouldn't be able to handle it."

Surprise covered Ann's expression. "Really?! Wow, that's serious."

"Well, so long as there's no pressure," Gail joked.

"Do you think he's in love with you?" Ann was apparently still wrapping her mind around what Gail was telling her.

"I'm pretty certain of it," Gail said. "And I think I'm in love with him, too."

Ann was so thrilled, she spontaneously leapt up. When she sat back down, next to Gail, grinning the width of the sky, she hugged Gail for what seemed like several minutes.

"I'm so happy for you."

Gail saw that she was crying.

"I definitely think you can make it," Ann said.

Chapter Twenty-Three

*D*avid and Devon Richardson strolled nonchalantly through the broken-down, old house, taking notes on every last detail and asking Eddie plenty of questions. Has the place been rewired? Yes, but you could probably use another circuit if you have any high-current requirements. Has the plumbing been replaced? Never. What about the roof? Ditto. You'll probably need to replace it at some point to keep it from leaking. Original plaster walls? Yes, except for the attic and bathroom, which were renovated more recently. Does the fireplace work? Yes, but you'll want to have a professional take a look at the chimney.

The Richardsons were a young couple in their twenties, with no kids and looking for a first home. Assuming they could scrape together the down payment, that made them prime candidates for a cheap but livable house. This one was the former, comparatively speaking, but not the latter, not by a stretch. They would find themselves needing to invest gobs of time and money in it, right from the get-go.

Eddie didn't have much faith that this would result in a sale. This wasn't a house he would buy; it wasn't a house he could recommend; and it surely wasn't a house any new family would want for their first home. Eddie was sure they would realize that, after they saw the extent of the repairs they would need to make and how much it would cost them.

But David's face lit up at each new problem Eddie pointed out. Maybe he was thinking that he could negotiate a lower price. And maybe they indeed could, because the owners seemed desperate to unload it. That wouldn't sell Devon, though, and she probably held the real purse strings.

But even she seemed pleased. She bubbled with joy that most floors and walls were original, and she was already talking about refinishing the former and patching and repainting the latter. The way she carried on, Eddie wondered if she already had wallpaper prints picked out and had just found a place to use them.

They finally finished the tour, with a list of action items, and with Eddie wondering what had just happened.

———

"You're a sweet girl, Ann, but impractical. We aren't running a charity here."

Gail was patronizing her now. Gail realized this, but she couldn't stop herself. It was as if an evil spirit had taken over her and was now controlling her words and thoughts.

When she had sat down to meet with Ann about the "non-payer issue," as Gail called it, she had intended it to be a constructive conversation. She had honestly gone into it wanting to understand more about what Ann really thought, assuming that this would help resolve their conflict. Instead, now sitting in the power position, with her business partner on the other side of her desk, Gail was fast discovering that every idiotic thing she had presumed Ann was thinking, was indeed what Ann had been thinking. And getting it all out into the open was just worsening the conflict.

This single meeting was completely destroying the pleasure she had experienced waking next to George that morning. They had stayed the night at Gail's, because they had not gotten back until long after dark. So together they cooked a simple but elegant dinner for two, just like in the old days, watched a movie, and fell asleep in each others' arms. Gail left for work before George had awoken, but she left him a love note, a fresh pot of coffee, and instructions for how to lock up when he left. She also asked him to call her when he got a chance. And she had been waiting since then to see whether he would call, to see how serious he was about her. Not that she doubted his sincerity, but she needed to know she had his strength to lean on.

Gail knew she had to continue her conversation with Ann, regardless of how it turned out, because the issue needed to be resolved, one way or the other. The experience was making her sick to her stomach, literally, made her feel like making friends with Mr. Tidy Bowl. And apparently, acting out at Ann was the only way to keep herself stable long enough not to lose it all over the carpet.

Ann said nothing. She just sat, looking beaten and sad.

Gail took a deep breath and decided to switch gears. "You know my other clinic, in Worcester."

Ann nodded, but looked even more disheartened.

"I've been wondering if I should move back there."

No comment from Ann.

"The last time I talked to them, they said they're doing fine, but I'm not sure I believe them. And they're my safety net if this place fails." She felt herself acting out again. Was she really that nervous about failure? Well, who wouldn't be?

Ann still said nothing.

But Gail needed advice, and more than that, she needed a reason to stay.

"I don't know," Gail said. "What do you think?"

Ann stared back cautiously. "Do you really want to know?"

"Yes." Straight-faced.

"My honest-to-goodness opinion?"

"Yes." Gail nodded soberly, a knot tightening in her stomach.

"I think you would be bored to tears if you moved back to Worcester. You came here looking for something, because Worcester wasn't fulfilling you anymore. That hasn't changed. Besides, it's probably best that they learn to manage on their own."

It was the most sensible thing Gail had heard all day.

"And," Ann added, "you've probably set them up so that they couldn't fail, even if they were complete incompetents... like me."

Gail had just wanted her partner to give in to her business advice, and Gail was beginning to see that her efforts had backfired. Truthfully, Ann was a skilled SLP, much more so than Gail, and she cared about her clients in a way Gail could only envy.

"I'm sorry," Gail said, staring at her desk. "I didn't mean to make you feel incompetent, because you're not." She looked Ann right in the eyes. "You're a better SLP than I'll ever be." Gail chuckled at the irony of her next thought. "That's probably why you're so determined on this issue." Because Ann, the object of her envy, cared about the people almost to the exclusion of the money.

And a little lightbulb switched on inside Gail's mind.

Ann showed some relief. "You could still visit Worcester occasionally, once a month maybe. That way you could help them with the odd problem, almost as a consultant."

Not everything Ann said was silly.

––––––

The call came as a surprise. Eddie was lounging around
at Gail's when his cell rang from David Richardson's
number.

As it turned out, David had connections in the
construction industry and had already been in contact
with a whole list of inspectors. Pending their reports, he
and his wife were ready to place a bid on the house.

In shock, Eddie told him that sounded fine. He would
be happy to coordinate with the listing agent.

Still in shock, he hung up. It took several minutes
before he realized that this sale could pay his expenses for
the next month. Longer than that, if he chilled it on the
dating and partying, and that was already, frankly, a fait
accompli.

But he needed just one more extravagance.

––––––

George popped the question when Gail least expected it.
They had been seeing each other steadily for a little over
2 months. They had been talking about what they wanted
out of life, probably for the first time in their lives. In
Gail, George found the excitement that he had lost. In
George, Gail found a challenge, sometimes just listening
and acknowledging his desires—and hers, too. But when
he listened to her, he always made her feel better, seemed

to instinctively know how to. She had forgotten that about him, and wondered why it had ever escaped them.

George plunged himself into Gail's world, as much as he could. And he began setting life goals of his own, starting with developing his skills as a real-estate agent.

He saw in Gail ever more of the fire for life and love that had originally attracted him to her, in her eyes, in her laugh, and especially whenever he saw her with one of her kids.

He even asked her what she thought of kids of her own. She had never really considered that, but if she was looking for new challenges...

"Maybe," she said.

George came to the office one Wednesday to take everyone out to lunch, supposedly to share his newfound good fortune, a huge commission on a two-family in Newton. He even invited Bob along and arranged to meet him there. He needed everyone there, including Bob. And then in the middle of everyone's coffee, he pulled out of thin air a blue-velvet jewelry box, opened it to reveal a sapphire ring studded with tiny diamonds.

"A simple diamond is simply not precious enough to symbolize what you mean to me," he said to Gail.

She shook her head. "No way. That's too extravagant a gift."

"Not under the circumstances," he said, and he got down on one knee. Taking her hand in his, "Will you marry me?"

———

Like most little girls, Gail had dreamed the perfect
wedding: a majestic chapel, red roses, white streamers; a
beautiful gown, a black tuxedo, and a host of friends and
family to share the occasion; a sparkling reception hall,
lavishly decorated and set with fine china and silverware;
then food, music, dancing, champaign, and more food and
music and dancing. She was going to avoid getting
slammed in the face with wedding cake, but she was
going to slam her husband—whoever he would turn out to
be—with that same cake; and everyone was going to
laugh when she did it.

The first time Gail married George, she got almost
everything she wanted in a wedding. It wasn't exactly as
she had imagined it as a little girl, but it was "perfect,"
and she was giddy with delight.

This time, however, all she wanted was a small cere-
mony, justice of the peace; or maybe her family minister,
if her mother insisted. And just her closest friends and
family in attendance: Bob and Ann, Mom and Dad and
Graham, and Mom and Dad Chase. And she wanted her
newly readopted parents to tell her again how much they
appreciated having her in the family. She didn't know
whether she would get that part, but of the rest she was
fairly confident.

When Gail called her parents with the news, Mom

nearly flipped. "Here we don't hear from you in God knows how long, and then you suddenly call out of the blue... with this?!" Or words to that effect.

Gail didn't know whether that was good or bad, and she was almost afraid to ask. But ask she did, as light-heartedly as she knew how, while applying the right amount of pressure. "What's wrong with that?" she joked. "I thought you'd be happy."

"Wrong?!" the word stabbing loudly into Gail's ear. "This is wonderful! I wish I could give you a hug."

Then Mom began making wedding plans, which Gail quickly put to rest. She explained what she wanted, and Mom seemed to take it in stride. But Gail let Mom keep the minister anyhow, just to ease the conscience.

But before Reverend Simpson would perform the cere-mony, he insisted that George and Gail attend marital counseling, and he even recommended several certified counsellors. If this had happened a couple years earlier, Gail would have kvetched, because she hated the idea of someone else telling her how to live her life. But now, even though things had been going well between them. Gail desperately wanted it to work and was willing to do whatever she needed to in order to make it work, and she needed reassurances. She welcomed the opportunity to talk to a professional. After all, whenever she hit hard times in her business, she sought out more experienced colleagues. That's how she learned to succeed. Why should her new— her *renewed* relationship be any different?

And that was how she felt, until she began to fear that he would tell them they were hopeless, or that they shouldn't get married, to forget about it, because she was afraid of what that would do to George. When they chose a woman counselor to visit, Gail felt a little easier, just with the thought of talking to a woman rather than a man. But she still worried about the outcome.

Easy-going George didn't feel one way or the other about counseling per se. But he was willing to do anything in his power to make the relationship work.

Waiting to meet their counselor for the first time, he saw that Gail was nervous. "What's wrong?"

Instead of answering him, she asked, "George, what if she tells us we shouldn't be getting married? Would you be okay?"

George grinned and kissed her on the forehead, as if she were a little girl. "If she tells us that, then we find someone else, because that's obviously the wrong advice."

But she didn't tell them that. Rather, she gave them good advice, taught them how to talk to each other, how to respect each others' space, how to connect with each other, how to include each other in their lives, how to prioritize the relationship, how to deal with stress, how to argue, how to fight fair, all core marriage skills. The question of whether or not they should get married never even came up.

For all intents and purposes, they were already married anyhow. All that was missing was the marriage certificate. They had been staying on and off at each other's domicile, and Gail had slowly been moving her belongings to George's house. She had even rearranged the furniture, hung new curtains, replaced her dishes for his, and installed an air freshener. When she awoke in the morning, weather permitting, she opened the windows and let the fresh air blow throughout. She made the coffee and loaded the dishwasher, but she asked George to take out the garbage when it got full. It was her home as much as his.

And she raged at his messes, cleaned up the dishes in the sink, scrubbed the toilet, and sorted through the opened mail from the past two years. It was all so familiar to her, but she never once said, "So *this* is why I divorced you," not even as a joke.

And while the average man might balk at this infringement on his property by his fiancée, it overjoyed George, because he had missed living with Gail, and he longed to again, to repeat the good things they had together.

So when George and Gail finally walked down the aisle, it was little more than a formality, the nine of them standing in front of Reverend Simpson, in an otherwise empty church. Afterward, they were to dine together, a family dinner at Bertucci's, good company, good food, nothing fancy. They had of course dressed up for the occasion, but nothing extravagant, no gowns, no tuxedoes. Just themselves.

Little more than a formality, but it still meant something. Particularly, it meant something to Gail, because despite the gradualness of it all, and despite the preparation, which had taken almost a year, that one moment cemented together her past, present, and future.

She and George kissed, turned to face their family and friends, and Reverend Simpson said, "I now introduce to you for the... *second* time ever, Mr. and Mrs. George and Gail Chase."

And someone played Mendelssohn's "Wedding March" from a CD. And George and Gail strolled, hand in hand, out to Gail's grey-gold Subaru. He opened the door for her, and he leaned over her and kissed her, a deep, passionate kiss. It reminded her of their blind date, except that this time he didn't apologize, and she had no doubts.

She hugged him, held him, and emotion overwhelmed her. She began to weep, and a tear trickled from her eye.

He didn't understand. He feared he had done or said something wrong. Wiping under her eye, "What is it?"

"I don't know. I guess I'm happy."

So he wrapped himself around her again, and they held each other until her tears became part of him, part of his past and his future.

"Why do you even love me?" she asked. "Why did you

love me, even when I was making a mess of things?"

"I love you because you're special to me, and that's enough. Besides, you're a wonderful woman. I don't know what mess you think you've made, but whatever it is, we all make mistakes— We've *both* made mistakes, too many to count, and none of that makes you worth any less or any less deserving of being loved."

*P*lease give feedback on this book. Positive or negative, every author needs readers to tell what they thought of his book. It will only take a few minutes of your time and costs you nothing, but will earn you appreciation from the author as well as self-satisfaction because you've contributed.

Here's how:

1. First, ask yourself:
   - What struck you the best about the book?
   - What struck you the worst about the book?
   - Do you plan to read more books in the series or by the same author?
   - How did the story make you feel?
   - What one biggest lesson, discovery, or new idea did you take away from the book?
2. Write the answers in a casual paragraph or two, as though telling a friend about the book.
3. Rate the book on a scale of 1 to 5 stars. Here's the rating system I use:
   - 1 star — The book upset me, and I loathed it.
   - 2 stars — Blech. I neither liked it nor hated it.
   - 3 stars — It was a good book, but I probably won't be reading more books like it.
   - 4 stars — I enjoyed the book, and I would like to read more books like it.
   - 5 stars — I feel loss for having finished the book, and I desperately long to read more books just like it, *right now*.

4. Post your review and rating on Amazon.com, BarnesAndNoble.com, GoodReads.com, books.LivingSocial.com, books.Google.com, or any other book sites you have an account on.

5. Post the review as a blog post on your blog.

Authors appreciate how meaningful reader reviews are. We know that readers don't always love our books, at least not as much as we love them. But always for an author, the challenge is to get noticed. And reader reviews not only help your favorite author get noticed, they'll also comfort him that people are indeed reading his books.

Jim

About the Author:

J. Timothy King is a stay-at-home father of two daughters, the husband of a wonderful wife, and an indie author of life-expanding, contemporary romance novels and other works. When not writing, he reads, plays bass guitar, and cares for his family in their Boston-area apartment.

Find more of his work at

http://www.JTimothyKing.com/